CONTENTS

| | |
|---|---|
| Chapter 1 | 1 |
| Chapter 2 | 13 |
| Chapter 3 | 15 |
| Chapter 4 | 27 |
| Chapter 5 | 37 |
| Chapter 6 | 51 |
| Chapter 7 | 65 |
| Chapter 8 | 83 |
| Chapter 9 | 95 |
| Chapter 10 | 113 |
| Chapter 11 | 123 |
| Chapter 12 | 141 |
| Chapter 13 | 157 |
| Chapter 14 | 175 |
| Chapter 15 | 187 |
| Chapter 16 | 199 |
| Chapter 17 | 219 |
| Chapter 18 | 233 |
| Chapter 19 | 251 |
| Chapter 20 | 257 |
| *About the Authors* | 267 |
| BALLS, TEQUILA AND TEA BAGS | 269 |
| *Also by Andie M. Long* | 271 |
| *Also By Laura Barnard* | 273 |

# Chapter 4

### Katy

*I*t wasn't the sight of my fiancé Richard's spotty arse, bouncing in the air like a trapped balloon in a tree on a windy day that made me erupt. Nor the fact that my non-identical twin sister Victoria appeared to be reaching the dizzy heights of orgasm, while laid underneath him; something I'd not managed in the last three years. No, it was the fact that lying on the bed at the side of them was my vibrator, and as my sister was about to find out once again, I did not share my toys.

'Don't mind me,' I shout in their direction. 'Just picking up a few things.' I drag my suitcase from the top of the wardrobe and put it at the side of them on the bed.

Richard, or as I've always thought matched him

better, Dick, has now turned his pale white backside away from my face and is looking between myself and Victoria. His face, in contrast to his bottom, is puce. His dick has shrivelled up so much, a newborn baby's would probably be as big.

'Erm, it's not what you think,' he blurts out pathetically.

Original.

'What?' My sister and I shout in unison.

I shove my case further onto the bed so he and my sister have to move up. My sister is glaring at Dick. Then she recovers herself and pats his knee.

'We've wanted to tell you for a while. Richard and I are in love.'

Of course they bloody are. Victoria wants everything I have, she always has. I won't let her know how gutted I am—that right now I'm not sure whether I should beat him to death with my vibrator or lock myself in the bathroom and sob.

'I'm very happy for you both.' I tell her, while throwing my undies in the case. 'Dick and Vic. I can see it embroidered on towels.'

'Do not call me -'

'Vic? Vic, Vic, Vic, pinched Katy's Dick.' I rhyme as we descend into the usual juvenile sparring that marred our parents' lives.

'I'm afraid you just didn't meet his needs.' She says with a smug smile.

Grrrr! The urge to pummel her in the face is strong.

'No. I wasn't prepared to put my finger up his rectum to get him to come or scream the words "do me now like the slutty whore I am".' I turn to him, wanting to hurt him. 'I have *never* had an orgasm with you.'

Dick looks at me with a smirk. 'There's no need to start lying.'

God, he's bloody sure of himself.

'I'm not lying. Cross my heart and hope to die, I have never had an orgasm with you.' My words are accompanied with the matching hand signal. 'I faked them all. She,' I jab my finger in Vic's direction, 'is probably faking. She's always been good at telling lies.'

Victoria's eyes blaze back at me. 'My orgasms are very real, as is my love for Richard. We want you to move out.'

I stop and gesticulate wildly with my hands over the case. 'What the fuck does it look like I'm doing?'

'Hang on,' says Dick. 'Shouldn't we talk about all this?'

'No.' My sister and I shout in unison.

I pull the zip around my case and stomp out of the house, slamming the door behind me. In this suitcase is all that I want right now. Mainly: my best lingerie, a decent amount of clothes and my Kindle. At twenty-six, this is how I find myself having to move back into my parents' house. All because of a Dick.

---

My mum has me sitting in their lounge with a blanket draped over me like I've been in a tragic accident. A cup of tea is thrust into my hand. My dad walks past me and strokes his hand down my dark brown hair, like he's comforting a lonely dog. They sit either side of me on the sofa. It's a good job my mum is tiny and slim as my ample backside makes it a tight squeeze. I might be twenty-six, but in my parents' eyes me and Vic are still about twelve. I am, but only in clothes.

'You two girls never could get along.' My dad shakes his head. 'I don't know what's wrong with that girl. She was always given exactly the same as you, yet she always wanted what you had as well.'

'It must be something to do with her being born second,' adds my mum, 'That's all I can think it is.'

'We love her as much as we love you, Katy, but sometimes I can honestly say I don't understand my other daughter,' says Dad. He offers me his shoulder, and I lay my head on it, welcoming the comfort my father provides.

'Can I move in here for a bit, just until I get a new place?' Luckily, Dick and I only rented, so I should be able to get my own place quite soon.

Dad looks to Mum, a frown wrinkling his forehead. I look to Mum. She's shaking her head. What the hell is going on here?

'Of course you can, sweetheart, it's just...'

'Just what?' I press.

'Well your mum and I didn't want to tell you girls until everything was official, but we exchanged today, so I suppose there's no time like the present.'

Exchanged? What the hell is he talking about? Have they got themselves involved in some weird kind of wife swap cult? They're too bloody naïve. I've been saying it for years. They'll be tied up in leather and lace, hanging from the ceiling before they politely consider it might be a bad idea.

He takes a deep breath, sitting up straighter, and clapping his hands together. 'We've sold the house.'

I can't help but stare back at him blankly. Like a complete idiot.

'Sold the house?' I repeat slowly.

They're selling our family home? Why the hell wasn't I consulted on this?

'That's right, sweetheart.' Mum says carefully. 'It's time for you girls to stand on your own two feet.'

'Our own two feet? I rent a flat. I'm hardly still living in the basement!'

'We just need to start enjoying our lives now.'

I fold my arms across my chest. 'What the hell was wrong with your lives before?'

'Katy,' she says more sternly. 'You have no idea how hard it has been raising twin girls. Especially with your rather spirited sister. We deserve this.'

I suppose I can understand that, but I can't help but feel like an unwanted burden. I always remember my mum smiling and laughing while we were growing up; not finding the whole thing a nightmare.

I take a deep breath and beg my tear ducts not to erupt. 'So... are you staying local?'

Mum looks to Dad. Dad grimaces. 'Not exactly,' he admits.

Oh Jesus.

'How far?'

'We're moving to Edinburgh.'

*Edinburgh?* I yell.

I can't fucking believe it! Right in my moment of need, my bastard parents decide to up sticks to Edinburgh. It's hardly down the road from Derby. And they've exchanged. That means they're moving soon, right? I better get my shit together.

That evening as my parents lapse into their usual evening ritual of back-to-back television programme watching, I go into my bedroom. They stripped it of all my Justin Timberlake posters (man, I wanted that trouser snake), but it's still painted pink and has glow-in-the-dark stars stuck to the ceiling that my dad moans he can't get off.

I peel back the duvet and slide down into the single bed. My room is the smallest, my sister having claimed the larger bedroom after a tantrum about having to share. I gave up as it wasn't worth the hassle. I've always given up. Given in. Well, not this time.

I look around at my teenage life before I went to uni while my eyes adjust to the darkness. Back home at my parent's house, in my small bedroom while Vic sleeps soundly in my bed, in my flat. I feel the pillow beneath my cheek get moist, so I turn over and let sleep take me some place else.

The next morning, I get ready for school. I'm an English teacher in the same high school I attended when I was younger. Talk about coming full circle. We're two months away from breaking up for summer vacation and I cannot wait.

I put on my work 'uniform' of grey, wide-leg trousers and a white tunic style top that covers my backside, and finish with a plain grey cardi. Then I tie my hair back in a high ponytail. I don't bother with any jewellery as we're only allowed stud earrings, and my skin is okay enough that I leave my make-up off too. I always prefer the extra twenty minutes in bed.

Despite my not wanting to stand out, I'm firm with the kids. I get to know them well and they respond to the boundaries I set them. Well, for the most part anyway. I slide my large bag off the table, along with an extra shopper filled with textbooks.

'See you later,' I shout up to the parents, whose own alarm has just gone off.

'Have you had some breakfast?' My dad shouts back. He's always on about it being the most important meal of the day.

'Gary, she's old enough to know she needs breakfast,' my mum says.

'Oh shut up,' I hear him reply. 'She's still my baby.'

I roll my eyes and with a smile on my face head out of the door.

---

My sister calls me at break-time. I hesitate but answer.

'What?'

'When are you going to pick up the rest of your things?' she snarls down the phone. No "hi". No, "sorry I stole your boyfriend, hope there's no bad feelings". Nope, straight in there with the kicker.

'For God's sake, Vic; I only caught you at it yesterday.'

'Yes, well I want to make this space mine and I can't do that with your stuff in it.'

How can I be related to this monster? I'm surprised she didn't try to eat me in the womb.

'Don't you mean you want to make the place *yours*? Yours and Dick's?'

'That's what I meant. I want to make it a home Richard will love rather than the student accommodation look it has right now.'

Rubbing my forehead, I sit on one of the battered

old sofas in the staff room. I'm close to breaking point with her now. I've never let her see she gets to me, but I love how I decorated my house: in whites with bright accessories. It has a Danish feel to it and the decorations in it are a personal touch; put there with care. An eclectic collection.

'I'll call for them tonight.'

I can hear the smirk in her tone down the phone as she replies 'fabulous.'

From somewhere deep within, I feel a tendril of red hot fury unfurl. I have never lost my temper with her, but I feel a root of pure evil start to release.

'Oh, and can you make sure the car's outside and the key's ready?' I add.

'I beg your pardon?'

'The car. The BMW. It's in my name.' I'd left in a taxi the night before, wanting to return and sort things out fairly, but it looks like that was never going to be an option.

'I want the car,' she says. It's as if I can hear the pout on her face.

'Well you can't have the car because it's mine, and if I see any damage to it—of any kind—when I come to pick it up, I will make Dick settle it. Which would come directly from your Dick Trussed-up fund.'

'Bitch,' she spits.

'That's right Vic-tor-ia.' I feel strangely energised by the feelings ignited within me. The anger is empowering. 'I want to thank you for starting this change process that's happening to me. I think it was entirely for the best. From now on you can call me Kat. Katy has left the building.'

'You've gone insane.'

'Maybe. But you need to watch out, sis, cos this new Kat has claws.'

Ending the call, I sit back on the sofa feeling really good inside. I stood up for myself and nothing bad happened. I need to do it more often. And that's when I see him, the one sicko in this place that's going to help me.

Not a marriage prospect. God, no. But the one for my new project. For no longer am I going to be the bloody goody-two-shoes I've always been before. This good girl is going bad and Felix Montague is going to help me get there.

I watch as he swaggers into the staff room because that's all it can be described as. He hardly picks his feet up from the floor. His hips flex, drawing in the soft pale-blue shirt he is wearing that pulls across his torso. I've overheard some of my colleagues state that under that shirt is a tattoo, a dragon, that snakes around his right arm and over his right pec. I've never had a dream about it. Never.

He walks right past me, doesn't even notice I'm here. I want to laugh out loud as he goes over to the coffee machine and Debbie falls over herself to ask him what he wants to drink. He winks at her as she passes him his mug and a wrapped chocolate biscuit, and then he flops onto another sofa. He runs a hand through his wavy brown hair, a shaggy style that matches his nature.

Felix has been at Ashfield School in Derby since the beginning of the school year. Long enough to have worked his way around half of the female staff —some married, some not—and long enough to have earned the nickname King Cock.

I decide to watch Grease this weekend for motivation. It's time for Sandra Dee to die and the kitty to come out of this Kat.

# Chapter 2

## Felix

Well, I'm guessing from the missing engagement ring that my mission is complete. Get revenge on that snooty little bitch that's been bad-mouthing me. I've always thought Katy a boring stick in the mud, but when word reached me that she'd been slagging me off at work, I was livid. It's one thing not to like me, but to put a doubt of my abilities in my workplace in peoples minds? Nuh-uh, not cool. And calling me a manwhore? That woman knows nothing about me. The rumours at work were just that—rumours. I haven't slept with anyone here; not that they haven't tried, but I get the feeling she'd never believe that.

So when I was having a cheeky pint after work and I overheard a guy bragging about doing his fiance's twin sister, my ears naturally perked up. I looked over him: medium build, shitty brown hair. He was nothing special. And he was doing it with twins. I was jealous as fuck.

When he started mentioning a Katy; at first, I was sure it was a coincidence. But hadn't I heard Grey at work joking that she was a twin and he'd love to be the meat in that sandwich? It was basically confirmed when he mentioned the school we both worked at.

His mate asked him when he was next seeing the cheating twin, and he eagerly told him they were having an afternooner the following lunchtime. I can't help that it just fell into my lap like that.

What I could have stopped myself doing was hacking the school email system, (which a toddler could do by the way), and sending her an email giving her an unexpected afternoon off. I made sure that she'd be walking in on them. I wanted her devastated; that smile wiped off her face. And by the look of things mission accomplished.

# Chapter 3

### KATY

*I* corner him after school. Well, corner him is a bit strong. Instead I lurk meekly by his door waiting for him to finish up and leave. God, he fannies around a lot for a dude. The door to his classroom finally opens and out saunters Felix Montague, the history teacher, and sex god. He looks even better at the end of the day, all pulled down tie and undone top button.

He spots me immediately. 'Katy,' he says in shock. He quickly composes himself. 'To what do I owe this pleasure?' He asks in his London accent, doing a stupid little bow like I'm the queen.

I suppose he must assume I'm a stuck-up bitch. I've always avoided him before now, having no time for dickwads like him. Players that are only interested in talking to you if you have huge tits and a fresh and tight vagina ready to go. No, thank you. Not that I don't have a tight vagina. I do. I could crack a walnut in there.

'Hi, Felix. I need your help.'

His eyes enlarge for a split second. 'Straight to the point, Miss Cornish. I like your style.' He smiles, his eyes dancing in amusement.

I can feel myself blush, which makes me angry. I don't want him to think for a split-second that he affects me in any way. He doesn't.

'Well, the truth is that my life is falling apart as we speak, and I need to do something reckless.'

'Reckless?' he smirks, seeming not to care for me to elaborate. 'Why?'

'I don't know,' I shrug. 'I've just always been the sensible one and I need someone to push me out of my comfort zone. You know, do something stupid for once? So I thought of you.'

'Me?' he scoffs, narrowing his eyes at me. 'Gee, thanks for the compliment.'

'Something makes me think you're not short of compliments around here.' We pass Mrs Sheldon who waves daintily while undressing him with her eyes. *Desperate whore. Go home to your husband!*

'So what you're saying is you want me to set a

dare for you?'

'Don't be silly. Are we about twelve?' I look at him, my forehead creasing. 'Basically, I have to pick my belongings up from my old home and I wondered if you'd pretend, just for the night, to be my new boyfriend?'

His mouth lifts in a smirk. 'If you want me to do you, babe, you only have to ask.'

'Oh my God, please stop or I may have to puke.' I adjust my ponytail. 'Look, I admit you're good looking and that's what I need. My sister has stolen my boyfriend and now she's kicking me out of my home. I want you to give me a lift there and just, like, put your arm around me or something. Then help me get my stuff and I can drive myself home in my own car. I'm collecting it from there.'

He's leaning against the wall, those brown eyes assessing me. He strokes his chin. 'Well, this is great and all that, but I don't see why I should help. What do I get out of the evening apart from a few pulled muscles from carrying your dictionaries and stamp collections?'

So that's the impression I give him. A stamp collector. Fucking fabulous.

I cross my arms across my chest. 'Well, what do you want? I'm not sleeping with you.'

'You said you want to do something reckless. I want to dare you, Miss Bloody Goody-Two-Shoes, to do something naughty. Something out of this comfort zone you say you're in.'

I chew on my lip while I think.

'And that's the only way you'll come with me tonight?'

'Yup.' He stares at me, eyes challenging. Why do I find the danger so enticing?

'Fine.' I nod, 'I'll do it. After we've been to my old home, you can set me a dare for tomorrow.'

Something tells me his imagination won't be able to conjure up anything too exciting or dangerous.

'Excellent. I'll meet you in the car park after school.' He pauses. 'How did you get here today then, if not in your car?'

'Two buses, both full of school children.'

He looks at me in sympathy. If there is a hell on earth, it's a school bus.

'Well, I'll be having a think about what I'm going to get you to do tomorrow.'

A feeling of premature regret creeps up my neck until it feels like it's strangling me. What the hell am I doing?

# ROAD TRIP

After school, I stroll towards the car park, in no rush to get this show on the road. Felix is waiting for me sitting behind the wheel of a bright red Mazda X5. He's such a cliché. He makes the top fold back. He might as well have just shown me his knob.

'Can you put that back up? An old boyfriend had a convertible once, and all I got was a fly in my eye and a trip to the local eye hospital.'

He snorts a laugh. 'God, you're a little ray of sunshine in my day, Cornish.'

'I just got dumped, like yesterday, and crossed by my evil twin, so excuse me if I'm not happy like a fucking bunny rabbit.' I get in and slam the door behind me.

'You have an evil twin? Does she look like you? Can I have her phone number?'

I exhale loudly and climb into the car. Felix begins to put the roof back on.

'You can't have her number because you're my boyfriend today and she likes to steal my things so you must never, ever, date her because then she'll win against me again and then I'd have to kill you and the poor kids learning history would fail their exams, all because you couldn't keep it in your pants. You've already affected Maths and Chemistry, let's leave it at that.'

'Those teachers got promotions.' He protests.

'Shortly after mooning over you and having a fist fight in the staff room. Sure they did.' I sit back in my seat and give him my old address.

'So tell me the story,' he says while starting the engine and putting the car in gear. We set off out of the car park and I don't fail to notice that a couple of female teachers have narrowed gazes as we leave. Great, the gossip mill will no doubt be in effect tonight.

'Well. I'd been with Richard, who we now call Dick by the way, for three years. Lived together for one, engaged for six months. No wedding plans made thank God. Yesterday I caught him shagging my sister.'

'Wow. Some sister.'

'Yep. She always covets what I have, so be on your guard because she'll get tired of Dick real quick once she sees you.'

'Everyone gets tired of other dick's when they see me.'

I try to sigh and perform an eye-roll, but he's too funny, and a giggle escapes me.

'She laughs. Thank God for that. You look so much prettier when you laugh.' He says.

I ignore him and focus on the journey. I know

he's trying to make me blush and I won't give him the satisfaction.

'So now my sister is moving into our shared rental and I'm moving out. Luckily it was furnished so other than my actual bought belongings, like ornaments and cushions etc, there should be just a few boxes. There are no large items to move.'

'Right, so that's all good to know, but I meant what's our story, our back story?'

'Oh, right.' I feel my cheeks flush a little. I'm such an idiot. So I just told him all the details of my personal life and that wasn't what he meant at all. 'Erm, we've loved each other from afar for months and now there's nothing stopping us from getting together. I have the moral high ground over Victoria and Dick because we haven't slept together yet, but I'm following you to your house, so we can have a bout of mad, passionate bonking.'

'Sure we can't do that instead and then go fetch your stuff. Add to the authenticity?'

I look at him with dagger eyes to find he's winking at me, his eyes dancing with mischief. I just shake my head at him.

'You are such a manwhore.'

He doesn't reply. Just goes quiet and checks the Sat Nav.

My sister's face is a fucking picture when she clocks Felix with his arm around me as she opens the door. I note my things are already packed in the sort of boxes you get from professional removers, and I know she's had someone do it for her. Richard's savings will be gone within a month with my sister. Not that I should give a toss.

'Hey, Vic.' I smile. 'Felix, sweetie, are you alright loading these in the back of my car?' I take my keys from Victoria's hand while she's still open-mouthed. 'I'll be putting the back seats down.'

'Only if later on you'll put those back seats back up for us to climb onto darlin'.' He winks at me and before I turn towards the car, he slaps my arse! I'm going to kill him when I next see him alone.

Victoria puts an arm up against the door jamb and extends a manicured hand. 'I'm sorry, we haven't been introduced. You are?'

Felix ignores her outstretched hand and pulls me in closer to him, nibbling my ear. It makes a shiver run all the way from my ear, down my spine, reaching my toes. Fuck, he doesn't know that my ear tip is a main erogenous zone for me.

'Hurry up and get that seat down, Katy, because

I'm getting a bit desperate to get you back to mine now.'

We finish loading up the car. Victoria disappeared for most of the time we were there having nothing to goad me about now she realised I had a "new man".

She says goodbye to us as if she's ridding herself of staff and closes the door in my face.

A few minutes later we've managed to pack all of the boxes into the back of my car.

'Your story is delivered. Her face looked like she'd swallowed a wasp. You're not at all alike, are you? Non-identical in almost every way.'

'Almost?'

'You look around the same height and weight.'

'Vic only eats steamed fish and salad. She takes after our dad; he's a bit portly. I think that's when she first started hating me, when she realised I was staying slim like our mum. If she ever pissed me off at home, I'd eat a four pack of Mars Bars in front of her face.'

'I'm seeing another side to you, Miss Cornish. A total fresh perspective and I like it.'

I close my boot and turn to Felix. 'Thanks so much for your help.' I tell him. 'Is she watching?' I ask.

'There's a shadow behind her bedroom curtain.' He tells me. 'So prepare yourself.'

I open my mouth to ask what he means when it's captured with his own. His lips crush against mine, soft and warm and although my mind is protesting *manwhore alert,* my body is saying *hell yeah*. I tell my mind that we're making Vic jealous and my body has a little happy dance inside.

I wrap my hands around Felix's neck pulling him further into me. His arms come around me so he's gripping my backside, pulling me towards him. I feel evidence of his hard-on against my own general girl parts area. Well, I wasn't expecting *that*! His tongue tangles with mine and I get the feeling he's making the most of his acting opportunity. The thing is, I have to ride out this snog because I can't be seen to be pushing him away.

So it's still happening, like it must have been about four minutes now. My girly parts are proper tingling and all because of this manwhore. It's not allowed. I'm trying my best for drool not to run out the corner of my lip, but it's going to happen soon if he doesn't quit. I try to talk while kissing but it just comes out sounding like a groan which makes him kiss me even harder.

Then the next minute we're soaking wet. As we

spring apart, I see Victoria standing there, hip cocked, arms folded, with an empty bucket at her side.

'I realised I'd not washed the car for you before you collected it. Sorry about that.' She says, before turning on her heel and walking off.

'What a bitch,' Felix says, water dripping down the line of his nose. I'm kind of listening but now his blue shirt is wet, and I can see his nipples through it and some of that tattoo. My traitorous mind is wondering what his body underneath it is like.

'Yep, bitch,' I reply, deciding I'd better look up.

'Right,' Felix coughs, his eyes fixing on mine. 'I'd better be off. I'll see you in the morning. Be prepared for your first dare.'

He leans in and kisses me, soft and deep once again. What the hell? Are we just kissing friends now?

'For your sister's benefit obviously,' he says as he walks off to his car. I go to get in mine and it's only when a cyclist passing me front on, almost falls of his bike that I realise my own white blouse has gone entirely see-through, giving passersby and Mr Montague a clear view of my tits.

## Katy

*I* wake up with butterflies in my stomach and a feeling of dread. I've got to do a dare. What the hell is Felix Montague going to make me do? He's already helped me with the furniture stuff now though, so if it's anything too horrible I'll just say no.

I dress in another pair of grey trousers and a black tunic top today. Full breakfast down me and parents reassured I'm fine, I'm on my way.

As I get out of my car, I see him get out of his own. He's been waiting for me. Clearly, he can't wait for me to be his puppet. Great. Not even time for another coffee before he descends.

As he approaches, I note he has two coffees in his

hand. One of them better be for me. I sigh to myself. Now the aroma is going to hit me. I may drool.

'Black, right? No sugar?' He hands one of the cups over to me.

*What the hell?*

'Erm, yes. How do you know that?'

'I've stood behind you in the staff room loads of times.' He smiles down at me. 'You always take your sweet time.'

Ah. Knew he'd follow it with an insult.

'Oh, yeah, right.'

'So,' he leans in, his smile smug, 'Are you ready for your first dare?'

'First?' I snap at him, taking a sip of the coffee. 'I agreed to one.'

'Yes, but if I give you the one I actually want you to do, you'll shit your pants, so we'll build you up.' I roll my eyes. 'Today I want you to do this.' He leans over and whispers in my ear.

*Get away from my erogenous zone*, I want to yell at him as his soft breath tickles my ear.

'Fine. I can do that.'

'Report back to me in the staff room at lunchtime,' he demands, clearly loving the small bit of power.

'Yes, Sir.' This time I do a sarcastic salute.

'Don't "Sir" me, I like it too much.' He does his usual wink/smirk combo and walks away.

---

Miss Chambers (Sarah) and Miss Jennings (Charlie) sit either side of me in the staff room as I sit nursing my third coffee of the day before I have to get to class. Funny how they're suddenly so interested in me; they've never been anything but colleagues who share polite conversation before. Yet they now sit here smiling at me like we've been best friends all our lives.

'Someone seems to be getting close to Mr Montague,' Charlie chirrups, raising an eyebrow at me that clearly says *"tell us your game plan, bitch"*.

Ah, so that's why they're suddenly interested. One of the others has obviously passed on that they saw me getting into his car last night. Add us walking into the staff room together and the rumour mill will be saying I'm having his illegitimate baby soon.

I pull a face. 'You've got to be kidding me. He's a dick. I needed to ask him something about a pupil that's all.'

'But you got in his car last night,' Sarah crosses one leg over the other and then flicks her hair back.

I shrug. 'My car had problems. He offered me a lift to the garage. I took it. He might be a dick, but he's better than the school bus.'

They mock shiver and I can see that they believe me. Of course, why would Mr Montague choose the traditional and uptight Miss Cornish over their designer-clad arses? It obviously makes more sense to them.

'I thought it was a bit strange as you'd never talked to him before, and of course you're—' She looks at the relevant finger of my left hand, no longer containing my engagement ring, and her voice trails off, 'engaged.'

Well I don't want to tell these nosy bitches what's happening in my private life.

'I am. But I'm having the stone cleaned at the moment.' I stand up, straightening down my trousers. 'Right excuse me, ladies. I need to get to class.'

With that I leave them to speculate further on whether I'm telling the truth or lying through my teeth.

A classroom of fifteen- and sixteen-year-olds is not my favourite thing, so I actually think this first prank will be fun. They like to think they can chat and text on their phone throughout the lesson and sometimes it's hard to keep their attention. This will confuse the fuck out of them. I have to stop myself doing an evil laugh.

I write all twenty-eight names down on my board with different numbers and symbols at the side of them. Total random crap.

The class wanders in and eventually all eyes are on the board, the girls overly filled-in eyebrows raised in confusion.

'What's that, Miss?' asks Brad, one of the gobshites in my class.

'I'll explain at the end of the lesson,' I tell him.

My class is the best behaved they've ever been. Heads down for the most part and work done. Every so often, I see a head pop up and look at the board, a face wearing a mask of puzzlement or a concerted effort to try to work out what it means.

Then we get to the end of the lesson and I wipe the board clean.

'Miss, what was it?' Brad asks again.

'It's just a shorthand thing I was experimenting with, to help me assess you. I've decided it doesn't work,' I tell them. 'Never mind, forget it.'

There are exhalations of relief around the classroom and once they've all left, I sit in my seat with my back to the room facing the blackboard and explode with laughter.

'Went well then, did it?' His southern voice comes from behind me.

I spin around in my chair, unable to hide my huge grin. 'That was glorious. I've never had such concentration in my class. Anyway, I thought I needed to find you at lunch?'

'I couldn't wait to find out if you'd done it or chickened out.'

It gives me a little thrill to think I've been on his mind. No, Katy. Don't fall for his charms. It was that kiss. He clearly attempted to suck the sense from me.

'Well, anyway. Don't come chat to me in the staff room. I have frenemies engaged. Your fan club think we got it going on.'

'To be honest,' he sits on top of a desk opposite me, releasing a sigh. 'That would do me a favour. Get them off my back.'

'Dream on,' I tell him. 'The heat would be off you and straight onto me. That's not happening any time soon. You made your bed and shagged in it. Man up.'

He frowns, staring at me intently. What the hell is up with him?

I look away, scared he'll hypnotise me somehow. 'Now what's my next dare?'

# ROAD TRIP

Over the following days, I cable tie shut the backpacks of all the girls who put their make-up on several times a day, causing a meltdown as their lip glosses wear off. I tell my students I'm disappointed with how many turned in their homework when I'd not set any. I give them a test to do with twenty English questions, neglecting to tell them to read the instructions carefully. The test instructions say only to answer the first question, so I'm delighted when everyone completes the whole test and I get to see their faces groan at the end of the lesson.

I tell them I've made them homemade brownies and then uncover a tub that has brown paper E's in it. That one made me really laugh. They didn't see the funny side.

By Tuesday of the following week, I tell Felix to give me the main prank because I want to return to teaching them properly, even though it has been fun.

'There is no way I'm having a mock fight with you in my classroom. No way.' I shout.

'Well, come do it in my classroom then. Mine are used to pranks.'

I huff. 'I bloody bet they are, with you as a teacher.'

'Gee, thanks.'

'No. We'll call it quits now. I've done some pranks, and you got my stuff with me, so it's all good.'

He looks at me sternly. 'It's not good because you've broken our agreement. You've not done my prank.'

I shrug my shoulders. 'Oh well.'

'Hmm, I think I'll be paying your sister a visit tonight. I'll tell her you were shit in bed and then ask her out. Or maybe I'll just tell her you lied all along.' He stands feet wide apart, his head tilted slightly.

Oh my God. The manipulative bastard.

'You wouldn't?'

I look at his face. He doesn't seem to be joking.

'Yes, yes you would, because you are Felix Montague, manwhore and douchebag.' I roll my head back, mock banging it into the wall behind me. 'Your classroom. When?'

---

The prank is set. Now all I have to do is come way out of my comfort zone and play my part.

I let my class out five minutes early. Not one of them says anything, they just rush for the door, obviously thinking I'm having some kind of nervous breakdown. Meanwhile, I hurry around the corner to Felix's class. My heart has been thudding in my chest all morning in anticipation. This is it. Time to play my part.

I take a deep breath and give myself a pep talk. *If you can do this Katy, you can do anything.*

I bang open the door so loudly, several teenagers jump from their seats. One of them is Brad the gobshite.

'I want a word with you.' I shout at Felix.

He drops his pen on the floor, in pretend shock. 'Miss Cornish, is everything all right?' A secret smile plays on the edges of his lips, only visible to me.

'No. It most certainly isn't all right!' I yell. 'How could you? That promotion was mine.'

He huffs and dramatically rolls his eyes. 'Didn't see your name on it.'

Show time.

I launch myself towards him, grabbing his shirt as I mock wrestle him to the ground. He yelps, and I realise I accidentally touched skin with my nails. All eyes are on us and voices rise as the children get up to gather around.

Felix pulls my ponytail which does actually sting a bit, so I dead-leg his thigh with my elbow. Fuck that was hard as a rock. The man's pure muscle. My elbow hurts.

'You're an idiot,' I yell for real as I nurse my elbow, my traitorous eyes running from the pain from that and the hair pulling.

Then I find myself pulled aside as a fist launches straight into Felix's jaw.

'Leave her the hell alone.'

I look to who threw the punch. Brad. Oh dear.

# Chapter 5

### Katy

Well that went well. Not. I got fired. Bloody fired! The first stupid things I do in my life and I get caught. Once I admitted it was a prank and that Brad shouldn't be punished for violence, the Headteacher said he had no choice but to let someone go.

Apparently, some kid streamed it live on Facebook, so the office was overrun with complaining parents ringing in, wanting something to be done. Someone's head on the chopping board. I tried my hardest to let it be Felix, and I blamed the whole thing on him and said I got led astray. I've already lost too much this week. Well it was Felix *and* me.

I do kind of feel bad that he lost his job too, but it's not like he was employee of the year beforehand. Whereas I've been a bloody star. Never late, always ready to take on more work, frequently bringing in Krispy Kremes. I should have been given a medal working with these fucktards for so long.

Only, well now that I'm looking for teaching jobs, there doesn't seem to be many. And by many, I mean any at all. I've had to expand my search to the whole of the UK and even then, I've only got ten interviews lined up. I have no idea how I'm going to drive all over the country to attend them but needs must. Mum and Dad have started packing up the house and I've been told I have only a week to get my stuff out. Charming.

Meanwhile that bitch of a sister has coasted through life, always landing on her feet. Well not anymore. I'm the Kat that's going to fall on her feet this time. I'm going to find an amazing job in a new part of the country, start afresh and be the new Kat that I've always wanted to be. It's just what I need.

I'm just packing my last few bits into my suitcase when the doorbell goes.

'Could you get that, love?' Dad shouts from their bedroom.

'No probs.' I pass him in his bedroom, as he attempts to dismantle his wardrobes. Mum's sat with a cup of tea watching him.

I run downstairs and swing the door open to find Felix Montague leaning against my doorframe, his hair more dishevelled than usual.

'Felix,' I say stupidly. 'What are you doing here?' And how did he know where I was staying. That's weird.

I look around him to see two black bags. Is it rubbish day?

He looks up at me, his eyes troubled. 'I need your help, Kat.'

I cross my arms over my chest. 'Why the hell would I help the person that got me fired at work?'

'I could be saying the same bloody thing to you!' he snaps.

Well he's got me there. I sigh. I'm too busy to fight right now.

'Do you want to come in?' I offer begrudgingly.

'Thanks,' he nods, seeming completely unaware it wasn't a genuine offer.

He picks up the two black sacks and carries them into the house.

'Err... why are you bringing our rubbish in?'

His shoulders sag. 'This isn't your rubbish. This is my fucking life.'

'Alright!' I hiss. 'My parents are upstairs, and they hate swearing.'

His face contorts. 'You're living with your parents?'

'Yes, just temporarily.' I fold my arms over my chest as if to protect myself from the humiliating truth. 'I didn't have much of a choice thanks to my darling sister. Now tell me why the hell you're here.'

His eyes droop, immediately turning into puppy dog, doe-eyed browns. 'I need your help.'

'Yeah, I heard that. Stop with the dramatics and just tell me.'

'Fine,' he hisses through clenched teeth. 'I need a place to stay.'

Is he for real? He wants to stay here?

'What? How the hell have you suddenly become homeless?'

He huffs. 'My landlord's selling up. I was all sorted to move straight into another flat, only then *someone*,' he pauses to glare at me, 'got me fired and now no landlord wants to take on an unemployed teacher.'

'So you're homeless? Why can't you move in with your parents?'

He scoffs. 'I don't know if you failed to notice my accent, but I come from down South. I'm a long way from home.'

'So go home then! It's what I've had to resort to doing. You might be proud, but there's no point you sleeping on the streets.'

He rolls his eyes. 'I know that. Which is why I'm asking to crash here tonight. Tomorrow I head home. Well, first I've got some interviews and then home.'

'Interviews?' I can't help but pry. 'Oh yeah, where?'

He puts his hand through his hair. 'All over the bloody shop. From Newcastle to Newquay. Who knew teaching jobs were so hard to come by? I thought they were desperate for us to teach the youth of tomorrow?'

Shit, is he taking the same interviews as me?

'So what you're saying is, I only have to put up with you until tomorrow and then you're going?'

'Yep. Out of your life forever.' He leans past me and grabs my printed itinerary. 'What's this?'

I go to grab it back, but he's easily a foot taller than me. Lanky bastard. I jump up in a feeble attempt to get it back off him.

'Give it back, Lurch!'

He puts his hand on my forehead, annoyingly managing to hold me back while his eyes scan over it.

'No way! You have the same interviews as me?'

'Do I?'

'Yeah. This is amazing. You can give me a lift.'

I splutter in shock. The cheek of this man is ridiculous.

'What?' I can't help but hold the revulsion clear in my face.

'Yeah, you've got a car, right? Mine was on lease. I've got to return it now I'm not earning. I was going to have to spend my last one hundred and fifty quid on train tickets. This is perfect. Road trip!'

'No! You honestly think I want to drive around the country with you? You're fucking insane!'

He steps forward, completely into my space. He places his index finger over my lips, his eyes brooding. 'Sssh,' he whispers. 'Your parents hate swearing.'

I hate how him being this close has my chest heaving up and down erratically. I hate that he affects me, and I hate even more that he knows it.

'If I do this for you, do you promise afterwards that I'll never have to see you again?'

He grins cockily. 'Darlin', it'd be my pleasure.'

'I'll make up the spare bed,' I tell him. 'After I've just checked it's okay with my parents.'

---

I should have known. My mother was out of bed by 6am the next day making a full English. I walked into the kitchen and there she was, hair done and fully made up. Then she looked disappointed to see me!

'Where's Felix?'

I shrugged. 'Either still in bed or with any luck he'll have changed his mind about staying here and left in the night.'

'Katy! That's not very charitable when you both got fired at the same time. You think you would have sympathy for your colleague.'

'Yes, you'd think so, wouldn't you?' Said the man himself walking into the kitchen.

Unlike me, who is still in a dressing gown over the top of pyjamas, with dishevelled hair; Felix is completely ready in his suit, looking like he's been lifted off the catwalk.

He holds out a hand towards my mother. 'Mrs Cornish. Thank you very much for letting me stay the night. I hope I haven't put you to any trouble.'

'Oh, it's no trouble at all.' Replies my mother, clasping onto his hand and then enfolding him in a hug. 'I'm sorry you got fired too. Times are dreadful at the moment, aren't they?'

He peers at me over her shoulder, raising an eyebrow in my direction and following it with a smug grin.

'They are. But hopefully I'll find something else soon and at least I'll have the pleasure of Katy's company as we head to the interviews.'

'Call me Marge please and... oh,' Mum looks at me with interest. 'You're traveling to the interviews together?'

'Yes, I looked at Katy's itinerary last night,' Felix says, while my eyes skirt over the kitchen table looking for my interview plan. Damn, looks like he's nabbed it again. 'We have the same interviews, so it makes sense for us to share one car and one lot of petrol. We'll have separate hotel rooms of course. She won't be getting her wicked way with me.'

My mum proceeds to laugh like a little girl, all tinkly giggles. God, she's embarrassing.

'Well, I think you should,' she says playfully with a wink. 'I've told her the best way to get over one man is to get under another."

*She seriously did not just say that.*

Felix makes an open-mouthed expression over her shoulder and mouths, "Oh my God."

*Yes, yes, she did say that.*

To someone whom she only thinks at worst is a colleague and at best a friend. Looks like she's desperate to get me married off, now things with Richard have gone tits up. It's only so I don't pester to move to Edinburgh with them and spoil their retirement plans. Pimping your own daughter out. That's desperate that is.

'Right, take a seat, Felix, and let me get this served up. You need to travel on a nice full stomach.'

*I am still here, right?* I pat my face. Yep, I'm present.

She puts us both a plate of food down, but Felix has double the portions I have. My mum eats a quick slice of toast and holds two cups of tea in her hands. 'I'm going to go back up to bed and take a cuppa up to your dad. What time are you leaving?'

'I thought around nine-thirty,' Felix says, as if he's organising the entire trip. 'Give the morning traffic a chance to clear.'

'Oh good idea, smart thinking,' Mum says with a nod.

'Well, we'll be down to say goodbye. If you want to leave anything to pick up in Edinburgh, Felix, if it makes things any easier for travelling, just leave them alongside Katy's boxes.'

'That's very kind, thank you.'

'You're welcome. It's been very nice to meet you, Felix, and you really should think about sharing accommodation. You don't have to sleep together, but it would halve your bills while neither of you have much in the way of finances coming in.'

Oh my God. This woman!

'Thanks, Mum,' I snap. 'We're sorted, honestly. Don't let Dad's tea go cold, he'll be grumpy.'

She looks at the cups in her hands as if she had totally forgotten they were there. 'Yes, better get these up. Well, catch you both later.'

I place my head in my hands. 'Please can you forget any of that just happened? Just think you took hallucinogenic drugs and now you're coming down.'

He snorts a laugh. 'I've taken them. They weren't half as trippy as your real life. Sister runs off with your husband-to-be. Your mother wants you to shag me already. If I didn't know any better, I'd say you were all sex maniacs. It's like a real-life soap opera being around you. Well, apart from the fact that you're so stiff. I'm actually surprised you're not still a virgin.' He pauses. 'You're not, are you?'

'No!' God, he's a buffoon. 'Now, interviews. Are we seriously travelling to them all, together? What if I get the job today? How will you get to the other interviews?'

'Ah, now this is a road trip remember?' The deal is, if anyone gets a job, the other still has to travel around with them all week. We *will* share digs. I'll take the sofa, I don't mind, because I really don't have the money for anything other than either a hostel, a cheap B&B or a budget hotel.'

'I've got a small bit of savings to go towards the week. Bit more than your one hundred and fifty quid, but not much. Maybe two-fifty.'

'So for the whole trip we've got four hundred quid? Jeez, looks like we'll be eating children's happy meals for tea.'

I shrug my shoulders. 'Beggars cannot be choosers.'

'So,' he holds out his hand. 'Road Trip. Together 'til the end. Deal?'

I grimace, but shake his hand, 'Deal.'

Why do I feel like I've just made a huge mistake?

All showered, packed and ready, we leave behind what we don't need, and I give my mum and dad a hug. Felix is now also loved by my dad. I swear he should bottle his pheromones for a new Lynx effect deodorant because everyone thinks he's bloody fabulous. He's like the Pied Piper, only with people, not rats. Unless you count my sister.

I take out my phone as I walk towards my car and tap on the keys, calling her.

'Hello, Victoria Cornish speaking,' she answers.

She fucking knows it's me. Bitch.

'Hi, Vic. I just wanted to say goodbye. I'm off on holiday for a week with Felix.'

'and I should care because...?'

'I just thought you should know that Mum and Dad are selling up and going to live in Edinburgh. They were going to ring you later, but I thought I'd give you a heads up, so it isn't as much of a shock when they call.'

'They're doing what?' she screeches.

'Yes, they're moving far, far, away, and there's no space in the new house for either of us apparently. So if you'd decided being with my ex is not as great as it first appeared, well, there's nowhere for you to go; unless you're going to get a place of your own.' I laugh uproariously at the concept of her doing anything by herself, for herself. 'So, Vic?'

'Yes?'

'Go suck a Dick.'

I end the call and throw my phone back in my handbag with a flourish.

'Well, Miss Cornish, I'm seeing a whole new side to you.' Felix gives me that smirk once more and I beam right back.

## Chapter 6

### Katy

'Right, I'm driving,' he says coolly, walking towards my car with a sports bag in one hand and one of my coffee mugs in the other.

'Err, first of all you're not bringing my coffee cup with you, and secondly, of course you're not driving, idiot. It's my car.'

'Yeah, but women drivers and all that,' he smirks.

Is he joking or is he seriously this deranged?

'Yeah, well it's ride with me or don't ride at all,' I snap, opening my car door to get in.

'I'm just used to doing the riding,' he adds with a wink as he gets in the car, still with my coffee mug, which on closer inspection says *Jesus loves you, everyone else thinks you're a twat*. A treasured present from Victoria. I have no idea why I ever kept it.

'Well, there'll be no riding of any sort going on during this trip. Understood?'

He salutes me like a soldier. 'Yes, sir.'

I cannot bloody believe I've somehow been talked into driving around with this plank. I mean seriously, how did I get so unlucky? Did I kill someone in a previous life? Victoria probably stole the luck right out of me in the womb too. I wouldn't put it past her.

'Right, where are we off to first?' he asks, his hand on the lever and pushing his car chair back so he can stretch his legs out.

I consult my list. 'First stop is Norfolk.' I start tapping the postcode into the Sat Nav. 'It says it will take us about three hours. Our interviews aren't until two pm and three pm, so we should have plenty of time.'

'You sure you don't want me to drive, so you can prepare for the interview?'

I scoff. 'Why on earth would I need to prepare? I'm already prepared. It's you that should straighten your tie and start working on your sales pitch. I doubt you'll be able to bed the interviewer. I was told it's a Mrs Amble. Doesn't sound like a ditsy blonde with huge tits.'

He rolls his eyes. 'I don't need to prepare anything. People naturally love me. It's you I'd be worried about. People assume you've got something stuck up your arse. You might want to look into that.'

My mouth drops open at the rudeness. 'There's still time for you to walk, you know?'

'Alright,' he chuckles. 'You won't hear another word out of me.'

And I don't. Nothing but loud obnoxious snores for the next two hours. I've tried shouting at him to shut up, but he only seems to stop for a second before starting again. That's quickly escalated to me slapping him in the face. I'm actually starting to worry. The guys out cold. If it weren't for the snores, I'd check his breathing.

I can't cope with this. Dick used to snore, but nothing to this degree. I'm just merging onto the M1 when I suddenly can't take it anymore. Felix fucking Montague needs to wake his arse up and NOW.

I swing my arm back and elbow him in the chest with such force that he blurts awake in a wild panic, eyes bulging out of his sockets, his arms flailing around so erratically he hits me away. My head hits the side of the door hard.

'Fuck!' I shout, the pain blinding me temporarily.

'Shit,' he hisses, as the car loses control. I feel myself flung around the car as he desperately attempts to take the wheel. I try too, slamming my foot on the brake.

We spin fast into a circle, the brakes screeching underneath me so that Felix's hard body is thrown into mine. I scrunch my eyes shut to stop the view of the road whizzing around me.

I'm going to die. *Oh my God, I'm going to die!*

It takes a few seconds of just hearing my own accelerated breathing to realise the car has stopped moving. I open my eyes slowly and look around. Felix is staring at me, eyes wide, clearly shaken.

'What the fuck, Kitty Kat?'

I stare back at him, my tongue quivering so much in my mouth I can't seem to form a response. He takes the wheel and starts steering it to the left.

'Accelerate slowly.'

I look around to see that we're in the left-hand lane and traffic is having to go around us. Slowly together we manage to get it on the hard shoulder. As soon as he pulls the handbrake up he turns to me, taking my shaking hand in his.

'Katy, are you okay?'

My throat tightens, emotion clawing at it.

Looking into his concerned eyes is too much for me right now. I burst into tears. Big, ugly, full-on snotty tears. He undoes my seat belt and pulls me into his chest, lifting me off my chair and over the handbrake onto his lap as if I weigh nothing at all.

He cradles me to him as I sob uncontrollably. I almost just killed us, all because I couldn't stand his snoring. What does that say about me? What does it say about my personality that his snoring grates on me that much? Maybe Felix is right, and I do have a stick up my arse.

'I'm sorry,' I sob.

He pulls me back to look at me, tilting up my chin with his index finger.

'What the hell happened back there? Did I...' his face twists in torment. 'Did I hit you in my sleep?'

Oh bless him, he thinks he's turned into a woman beater in his slumber.

'I hit you first,' I admit begrudgingly. He frowns back at me. 'It's just that you snore so fucking bad. Has anyone ever told you that before?'

'No,' he says in horror. 'I don't bloody snore.'

'You do! You're like a foghorn. Maybe it's just because you kick your skanks out right after sex and don't give them the pleasure of staying the night to hear your horrendous snoring.'

His face twists. Why does he look so angry?

'I don't sleep with skanks,' he snaps, completely removing his arms from around me. 'I'm driving.' He gets out, leaving me to fall into the seat and slams the door behind him. Well... that's upset him.

He goes around to the driver's seat and lets himself in, completely ignoring me. Why do I feel so terrible? He does sleep with skanks, right?

---

I thought driving with Felix would be hard work, but I never banked on him giving me the silent treatment. Normally he's a right chatty bastard. I can't have offended him that much, can I? Or maybe he is rightly moody due the fact that I nearly killed him. God, what was I thinking?

Anyway, I need to focus. We've just pulled into Norfolk and Felix's interview is in an hour. My stomach rumbles, reminding me that I haven't eaten since breakfast. I suppose nearly killing yourself will make you forget about your stomach. Well, only for so long in my case.

'Can we pull over somewhere and get something to eat?'

He nods, without saying a word.

'Shall we just grab a maccy d's?'

'Yeah fine. Suppose it'll help the budget.'

I find the nearest one using my map app on my phone and he parks up. We start queuing up with him still ignoring me. I've had enough of this crap.

I poke him in the shoulder. 'So are you going to ignore me all day or what?'

He sighs. 'Well I'm sorry if I'm a little pissed off that you almost killed us.'

'Was it really that? Or just that I intimated you were a manwhore?'

He rolls his eyes. 'Did you ever just consider that I could be nervous?'

'Nervous?' I blurt out in shock. 'Nervous of what?'

He rolls his eyes. 'If you must know, I haven't had an interview for a year and I'm hoping they don't ask any stupid questions.'

'Like what?'

'Like what bloody animal I think I'd be.'

I snort out a laugh. 'Well if it helps I reckon you'd be a cheater.'

He looks offended. 'Hey, don't put all us men in the same category as your ex.'

'Oh really?' I laugh. 'Coming from the manwhore.'

'Hey, I might have slept with a few women, but I don't cheat when I'm in a relationship.'

'That's because you don't have relationships,' I counter with a smug smile.

He grins, breaking the tension. 'True.'

We finally make it to the counter and put our order in. I decide to treat myself to a McFlurry too. The lady gives us our meal on a tray but tells me I have to wait for the McFlurry as there's something wrong with the machine. Isn't there bloody always?

Felix takes the food and wanders off to find us a table while I wait behind. God, I'd tell them to forget it, if it wasn't my favourite dessert. The woman finally places it down at the counter before running off to serve someone else.

I reach out to pick it up, but it's whipped away from me right before my eyes. I turn around to see a teenage girl about to walk away with it.

'Hey!' I shout aggressively. 'That's my McFlurry!'

She turns, a devilish smile on her lips. 'I don't think so. This is my McFlurry.'

'Well then you must be bloody blind, because that woman just handed it over to me.'

She shrugs. 'Finders keepers, bitch.'

She turns around and starts to walk away. The fucking cheek of it!

Before I even consider what I'm doing, I grab her arm and pull her back. She stares at me in horror.

'Listen here, you little bitch. I've already had the week from hell. I've been cheated on, fired, and now the one thing I'm looking forward to has been taken away from me by you. Not happening, sweetheart.'

I grab the McFlurry out of her hands. She attempts to grab it back and almost instantly we're playing tug-of-war with it.

Felix appears. 'Kat, what the hell are you doing?'

'This bitch is trying to take my McFlurry!' I shout, just as I lose my footing and the girl and I both topple over onto the floor.

He tries to intervene, attempting to take the McFlurry off both of us, but instead his strong hands force the ice-cream to shoot up and onto his suit jacket shoulder, and his chin. Oh crap.

I stare at him in horror, eyes wide. 'Oh my God. I'm so sorry.'

'Jesus, Kitty Kat. I've heard of women creaming themselves around me, but this is ridiculous.'

'I still can't believe I'm going to have to walk in with a stained jacket,' Felix moans as we wait in the reception area of the school.

'Oh shut up moaning about it, will you? I'm embarrassed enough.'

He smirks. 'I still can't believe you had it in you, Kitty Kat. Who knew you had claws? It just took a love for ice-cream to bring it out.'

I smile despite feeling pissed off. He has that effect on me. 'Just don't ever get in the way of me and my desserts and we'll get along just fine.'

He's the first one to be called, by a tall woman in her early fifties. He saunters in like he doesn't have a care in the world, when I know he's nervous. Who knew someone as cocky as him actually felt nerves? I suppose there's still a lot I have to learn about Felix Montague.

He emerges forty minutes later with the usual cocky grin I've become accustomed to. It still gives me a girly thrill when It's aimed at me. He gives me a discreet thumbs-up behind the woman. Well he obviously aced it.

'Katy Cornish?' the woman asks me.

I nod, with a large swallow. Now it's my turn, I feel ridiculously nervous. I've never been good at interviews.

I follow her in and sit across from her. She looks a bit flushed actually. That's what you get for spending forty minutes with Felix. Flushed. Not that he affects me like that. Of course not.

The interview goes well. I'm not as nervous and awkward as I'd feared and I'm feeling pretty confident by the end that I could be in with a chance of getting the role. Ha, that would piss Felix off.

The door suddenly bursts open and a scared looking secretary comes in. 'I'm so sorry, Mrs Amble, but your daughter has said she needs to see you urgently.'

She's pushed aside by a teenage girl who stomps past me and straight to her mother. Oh dear Jesus! It's the girl I was wrestling with over a McFlurry only a few hours earlier.

Shit, shit, shit.

Maybe if I keep my head down she won't notice me?

'Mum, Miss Philips is picking on me again. I'm telling you, you need to fire that bitch.'

Mrs Amble's face reddens, obviously embarrassed for it to have happened in front of me.

'Darling, this is something we need to discuss later. I'm interviewing right now.' She points to me as if to prove her point.

I discreetly nod, keeping my eyes on the floor. I can't help but take a peek and the little bitch is staring at me with recognition. Damn it!

'You're interviewing *her*?' she asks in disgust.

Mrs Amble looks at her daughter confused. 'Yes. Have you already met Miss Cornish?'

Here she goes. An evil smirk spreads over her lips.

'You could say that. She assaulted me earlier.'

Mrs Amble's mouth drops open, practically touching the floor. 'What?'

Okay, how am I going to play this? Think Katy. I'll feign ignorance and claim it wasn't me.

I pointedly look behind me. 'Sorry, do you mean me?' I ask as innocently as I can.

'Yes, you!' she shouts. She turns back to her mum. 'This woman is a nutter. Do NOT hire her.'

'You must have me confused with someone else,' I offer with a shake of my head. 'You hear about teenagers getting confused all the time. It's your hormones.'

She jumps into my face. 'I know it was you, bitch!'

God, she's aggressive for a young one. Maybe I don't want to work here if this is what the calibre of teenagers are like.

'Just admit it!' she screams, her eyes bulging out of their sockets. Jesus, is she on coke or something?

In that moment I want to smash her face in. I feel everything I've been through in the past week bubble up inside me. Getting cheated on, my own sister betraying me, losing my job, my parents moving away, having to travel with Felix. It bubbles until it hits boiling point.

'You stole my McFlurry!' I scream back, so loudly it echoes off the walls.

Silence descends on the room.

Uh-oh. That was definitely not the right way to react.

# Chapter 7

### Katy

'I can't believe it's straight back on the road, I'm knackered.' I complain, my eyes heavy and sore.

'Well, maybe if you hadn't been brawling you'd have more energy,' Felix fires back. Smart arse.

'So, it's five pm and the route planner says three and a half hours travelling so we'd better get on our way. I'll start driving and you have a nap. Then you can take over halfway.'

'Sounds good,' I tell him. After the drama of earlier I'm in no great rush to get behind the wheel again.

'What are we going to do about food?' He asks me. God, men, all they think about is either their stomachs or their dicks.

'No idea. Needs to be cheap.' I bite my lip while I think. 'I know, lets pop into a supermarket when we get a bit nearer and raid the reduced section.'

'Bargain old food it is. I can hardly wait.' Felix moans as we get into the car and he starts driving.

Of course, what we had not factored into the journey is tea-time traffic. In an hour we've moved what the Sat Nav estimated would take fifteen minutes. I now wish I'd not drunk a bottle full of water after my interview. It wasn't my fault my throat was so dry. It was the interview and then trying to get away from the stupid McFlurry stealing bitch.

Needless to say, I won't be accepting a job there should they offer me one, which they won't because I may have been dragged out of the room by Felix when Mrs Amble said everything could be settled by my apologising to her daughter. For which I shouted I would not be apologising to a McFlurry stealing brat, and I hoped that she was better at controlling schoolchildren than she was her daughter. Oops.

Mrs Amble was about ready to grab my hair for insulting her and her delightful daughter when Felix came in and daughter dearest said the ice-cream on his jacket was hers and proceeded to try to lick it off.

At which point her mother dragged her off while Felix got hold of me. We left in haste.

Now we're stuck in a traffic jam when I'd asked Felix if we could nip down to the coast and enjoy an ice-cream beforehand. But oh no, "We need to be on our way", he'd said, so now here we were, stuck in my car: no ice-cream, no beach, and with my desperate need to piss.

'I need to pee,' I tell him.

He turns to me. 'Well, we're nose to tail. Why don't you nip out and go behind the bushes? I won't have gone far.'

'I am not peeing behind bushes! And anyway, what if the traffic clears and then I'm stuck out here while you've gone off in my car? Or what if a bee stings my arse cheek?'

Flashbacks of Charlotte Jensen's sixteenth birthday play back in my mind. That damn bee. I couldn't sit down for a week.

'Don't be stupid, Katy.' He looks at me with furrowed brows. 'Oh God, it happened didn't it? Only to you. It could happen only to you.'

'It wasn't my fault, it was Victoria's.' I huff. 'She hit it with a stick while I was at a swimming pool party. It flew around and stung my bum. Then it died, so I felt really sad while Vic laughed that it had been so scared of my bottom it had died of fright.'

I could tell that Felix was trying very hard not to burst out laughing. Bastard. 'How old were you when this happened?'

'Fifteen. And I will never pee in the open air because of it.' I cross my arms over my chest so he knows I mean it.

'Well, I don't know what else we'll pass, but there are some services in two hours. Well, two hours plus traffic jam time.'

'TWO HOURS! I can't wait another two minutes.' My bladder is so bursting full it feels like it's going to split in two at any moment.

'Grass it is then.' He nods towards the bank in challenge. 'Look, I'll pull in to a layby when we get to one and you can use the car as cover.'

I pick up my water bottle. 'Do you think I could get it in here?' I ponder. God, guys have it so much easier with their dicks. 'No, that's disgusting. I can't do it.'

'It's not a fucking SHEWEE, but stop being so goddamn uptight woman. If you need to piss, get it in the bottle. Pretend I'm a doctor and I've asked you to provide a urine specimen.'

I huff, 'Definitely can't do it now. You made me remember that when I do wee samples, I get wee all over my hands.'

'God help me,' Felix says, looking up at the roof of the car.

After another thirty excruciating minutes, Felix pulls into a layby. My hesitancy about peeing in the grass has worn off due to the fact that I'm afraid that I'll explode and cover Felix and my car interior in a golden shower at any moment.

I dash into the grass, lowering my pants down as I hover. My stream starts with a gush. Boy, I really did need to wee, and the feeling is akin to an intense orgasm. It's *that* good. Not that I've had too many with Dick.

It's then I hear the buzzing. What the fuck? My luck can't be that bad, right? I must be having some kind of panic-induced flashback instead.

I grab my knickers and drag them up quickly anyway, but it's as the material touches my skin that I feel the piercing sting. Motherfucker!

'Ouch, fucking ouch. Oh my God,' I scream, pulling my knickers down to find a dying bee. Well that's what you get when you go around stinging innocent victims arses. God, the pain throbs uncontrollably. I run for the car leaving my pants in my wake.

'What the fuck is the matter with you now?' Felix asks, shaking his head as I run towards him. 'I know you're desperate for me but running towards me knicker-less is a tad desperate.'

'Shut up, you dickhead! I've been stung on my arse again. Felix, help me, it burns.' I shriek as I catch up to the side of the car.

'You will not have been stung, you're just panicking.' He says, as tears fall down my face.

'I have. Felix it really hurts. The sting is probably still in it. You're going to have to look and take it out.'

His jaw drops. 'You want me to look at your naked ass in a layby on the A17? We're not going to make tomorrow's interviews, we're going to be arrested!'

Hearty tears now pour down my cheeks and drip off my chin. 'I've never been so embarrassed in my whole life. Oh, I want to die.' I wail dramatically.

'Now, come on, Katy.' Felix pats me on the shoulder. 'It's not that bad. Come on then, let me take a look. You are not going to die.'

'I am going to die.' I state. 'Of embarrassment.'

He looks at me sternly. 'Katy, I work with

teenagers; I've seen worse things than your naked bum, let me tell you.'

'That would help,' I sniffle.

'What would?'

'Tell me about one of the much worse things you've seen while you check my bottom.'

Felix takes his wallet from his pocket and I watch as he lifts out a condom.

'What the fuck are you doing?' I shout. 'You don't need a condom to look at my bum. Are you trying to take advantage of me?'

He slips the condom back in his wallet and takes out a credit card. 'I'm moving it, so I can get to this card, which I need to help me take out the sting.' His eyes narrow. 'I don't need to take advantage of you. Women beg me to bed them. I don't have to attack them. I'm not a fucking rapist.'

'I'm sorry, I panicked. Please, Felix, can you look at my bum?'

A sentence I never thought I'd say.

Felix uses the car door to shield me a little and then yanks me hastily over his knee. He takes the hem of my skirt and lifts it up. I hear the intake of breath.

'Shit, you have been stung.'

'No shit, Sherlock.' I shout in frustration. I

cannot believe he's looking at my bare arse right now. This is too cringy.

'You can be a real moody cow; do you know that?' He tells me, giving my pain free arse cheek a little slap. 'Bad girl.'

I yelp. 'I swear to fucking God, Felix! Try that again and I'll fucking kill you in your sleep!'

'Okay, okay.'

He gets the sting out using his card, which is obviously his revenge for my mood. Tears spring back into my eyes, but it already feels a bit better.

'All done,' he says clapping his hands together. 'We'll get some antiseptic ointment when we get to the supermarket. It's a little swollen but hopefully it'll go down in a few hours.'

We get back in the car. I have to face the journey sat in a weird side on position as it's too painful to sit on my butt. I end up with a cramped neck. We eventually get to a supermarket after two and a bit hours and Felix, determined to drive all the way because of my "disability", insists we go to get food, drink, and cream.

'Found it,' he says, holding the antiseptic cream up for me. 'Now Dr Montague says to bend over while I apply it.'

I grab the tube off him. 'In your fucking dreams. I

can do it myself. That will be the first and last time you see my arse.'

We load up on reduced price sandwiches, cheap crisps, drinks, and a couple of reduced pastries. Once we've paid, I take my antiseptic cream and call into the supermarket toilets to freshen up. I use my handbag mirror to check out the swollen lump on my ass cheek. Talk about sexy. Only then I remember, I don't need to be sexy. I'm with the manwhore. I need to repel him. Showing him my arse probably wasn't the best way to communicate that.

On the way out, I buy insect repellent to keep bees away from my body and hope it has the extra special effect to stop Felix from bugging me.

---

We eventually arrive at a budget hotel at quarter past ten. This has been a long-arsed trip, well, actually a swollen-arsed trip. We arrive at the reception and ask for a twin room.

'We only have one double room left. There's been a convention nearby,' the woman says, uninterested, not even making eye contact.

Felix takes over. 'That's fine, we'll take it.' He looks at me, 'Got a problem with that, sweetheart?'

I shake my head, 'No, honeybun.'

When we get in the room and dump our belongings, I turn to him with a hand on my hip. I need to be strong and firm about this. Kind of like his biceps. No Katy, don't get distracted.

'So, what are the sleeping arrangements? Because there's no way I'm sharing a bed with a manwhore.'

He rolls his eyes before dropping down backwards onto the bed. 'Sleep in the car then.'

'Pardon?'

He fixes me with a death glare. 'Sleep. In. The. Car.'

'I heard what you said. I just can't believe you'd suggest that. What a gentleman. I thought you'd offer to sleep on the couch. That's what you said before.'

'But I'm not a gentleman, am I?' He spits out. 'As you keep saying, I'm a *manwhore*. So maybe you'd be safer locked in your car, so I don't come over all amorous in the night and shag you senseless.' He points to the couch. 'And my six-foot body does not fit on that. I'm sleeping in the bed.'

'But that's not fair!' I whine. I would have thought he'd have taken pity on me, what with my arse injury.

'There's room for two. We can stick to our own sides. I don't see the problem.'

'Well, I'll take the couch.' I grumble. Rather that than give him the wrong idea.

I start to unpack my things, laying my interview outfit over the back of the wardrobe door.

'I'll have to get my suit dry cleaned,' he grumbles, looking at the ice-cream stain. 'I hope they can get it done for the morning.' He picks up the telephone and calls reception. After making his request, his face darkens, 'You can't? Four pm cut off? Okay, thanks anyway.' He puts down the phone. 'Fuck. They can't do it.'

'Hey, give it here and I'll sponge it off for you.' I offer. 'I was always cleaning up after Dick.'

Felix snorts.

I narrow my eyes, 'I can always withdraw my offer.'

'No, please. Try to get the stain out. It doesn't give a great first impression to arrive with a white stain on your jacket.'

'Could have been worse, could have been on your trousers,' I quip.

'Except I also clean up after my dick,' He quips back.

I walk into the bathroom shaking my head.

When I get in there, I realise I've offered to miraculously clean his clothes when I have no wash powder, fabric conditioner, or a washing machine. Instead, I get my bath sponge from my wash bag, apply a little strawberry shortcake shower gel and rub at the offending article. It seems to do the trick. I gently rinse off the soap and then having rinsed out and squeezed my sponge I give it another last gentle rub and hang it over the shower curtain rail.

I come out of the bathroom looking triumphant. 'All sorted.' I tell him.

He smiles back gratefully. 'Thanks.'

I stare at the clock. It's now eleven pm, but I'm not the slightest bit tired and in fact, having been cooped up in the car most of the day I actually want to go outside.

'Shall we go have a wander around York centre?' I ask Felix. 'I know the bars are closed but we could get some fresh air and wander down the cobbles.'

'Why not?' he says with a casual shrug. 'I'll just change into something more comfortable.' He strips off in front of my eyes down to his boxer shorts in what feels like milliseconds. The bloke just does not give a shit. I would have excused myself and gone to the bathroom but oh no, not the manwhore. I find my eyes keep looking at his toned biceps, those broad shoulders, and that 'v' that dips into his boxers. Damn, that man is sexy.

I look for the rumoured snake tattoo and instead just find a British Bulldog. It's... well it's cute. Hardly the sexy snake I was imagining though.

'I like your tattoo,' I say, to cover up staring at him as he shrugs on some jeans and a tee.

'Thanks. It was a dare when I was eighteen. Right, I'm ready.'

I realise that I stood watching him dress when I should have been getting changed myself. I head to the bathroom and also put on jeans and a tee.

'Let's go.'

We reach the centre and stroll around looking in the shop windows and feeling sad that we've missed out on an alcoholic beverage. We walk down the length of The Shambles, admiring the cobbled streets and I window shop a little. When we reach the bottom, there's a crowd of people gathered.

'What's happening?' I ask Felix, my eyes wide with interest.

'Erm.' He places his fingers to his temples, 'nope, my psychic abilities have switched off. Damn the fuckers, how embarrassing.'

This man is bloody infuriating. I'm beginning to think begging Dick to take me back would be preferable to Felix-torture. Maybe I could enter a polyamorous relationship with Dick and Vic? Right, now I feel sick. God, I'm a poet and I didn't know it.

I decide to embrace my new 'me' and head toward the crowd. I'm getting brave, or stupid. Let's go with brave.

'What are you doing?' Shouts Felix to my back.

'Daring myself to be brave.' I shout back.

When I get to the crowd, there's a bloke dressed in olden day clothing. 'Cutting it fine, love. You wanting to join the tour? It's only a fiver.'

'What tour?' I ask him.

'The ghost tour.' He looks at me strangely.

Felix hands over a tenner. 'Yep, that's for the two of us.' Then he stands at the back.

I walk over to him. 'What are you doing? We're on a budget here.'

'We need to make sure that while we budget, we also have some fun, otherwise this is going to be a bloody long week. I can't expect you to get your arse cheek stung every night for my entertainment.'

I thump his arm.

'Violence.' He shouts out. 'Help me everyone, she's always hitting me.'

'Shut up. Oh my God.' I look at the faces around

me, some foreheads furrowing. 'He's joking. He has a stupid sense of humour.' We start walking along.

The supposed ghost tour turns out to be a history lesson: a long-arsed, boring as fuck history lesson. 'We could have bought wine, and shared chips,' I torment Felix. 'Instead, I'm bored shitless.'

'That so? Then I think it's time for a dare,' says Felix, a mischievous glint in his eye just visible from the street lights.

'Bring it.'

He whispers in my ear.

'Love it.' I tell him and then I instruct him on what we're doing after the dare.

The tour guide takes us to a particularly dark corner with some derelict houses and weaves a tale about hauntings and ghost sightings.

I walk over to an emo guy who looks to be in his twenties. He nods at me as I stand next to him.

'You can see me?' I say in pretend shock.

'Y-yes. Why would I not see you?' He asks me in confusion.

I turn to the others and shout out. 'Can you all see me? I'm a ghost. Can you all hear me?' Then I emit an ear-piercing scream that none of them were expecting. Several members of the crowd emit their own screams.

I cackle with laughter just before me and Felix leg it down one of the side roads leaving the rest of them to their boring tour.

'That was epic,' Felix laughs. 'Well played.'

'Yeah, well tonight I say fuck it,' I tell him. 'After that crap I need a beer. Let's head into Tesco Metro and treat ourselves to the cheapest shit they have.'

---

We change into our pjs as soon as we get back to the hotel. I go into the bathroom again to save my modesty. I leave on my bra and have on long-sleeved and long-legged pyjamas that keep me well covered up.

On exit I find Felix has left on his t-shirt and changed into some joggers. We enjoy our beers and finally the day catches up and tiredness hits.

'It's okay for you to share the bed, seriously.' Felix offers.

'I'm fine over here.' I say from the couch.

Drinks drunk, teeth brushed, I lie on the sofa with an extra duvet from the wardrobe over myself and a spare pillow beneath my head.

'Night, Kitty Kat,' says Felix. 'It was actually cool

to have some company today, even if we didn't get a job from it.'

Is he giving me a compliment?

'We have tomorrow,' I tell him. 'I think tomorrow will be better.'

Sometimes I should shut the fuck up.

# Chapter 8

## Katy

The first problem I have is the couch. There's a spring I'd not noticed when I'd been sitting on it, but it's very noticeable now. No matter what position I try it's sticking in my abdomen. Then of course there's my bee sting, the pain of which is lessening but still present.

I clock watch until it gets to three forty-five. We've set the alarm for seven to give us plenty of time to have breakfast and get ready. Just over three hours. Felix basically seemed to turn over and fall asleep immediately. He's facing the wall away from where I would lay. Maybe, I should slide in the bed after all and try to catch some zzzzz's?

I have a quick wee and then slide under the warm, toasty duvet, keeping right to the edge so as not to touch him. God, this mattress is like heaven compared to that sofa. I look one final time at the hotel's digital alarm clock set for the morning and finally sink into a blissful sleep.

'What the fuck? Katyyyyy! We're going to be late.'

I hear it from the floor because as Felix reached for the clock he knocked me out of bed.

THUD.

I bang my mouth on the edge of the bedside table on my way down.

'Arrrrrrggghhhhh.' I clutch my mouth. Oh my fucking God, the pain.

The light goes on and Felix peers down at me from the bed. 'Katy. What are you doing on the floor?'

'You fucking knocked me out of bed, cretin.' I mumble through my hand.

'But you weren't in the bed.' He looks so adorably confused right now.

'I got in at four am. I couldn't sleep.'

He raises his hands, 'Well, how was I to know that? Anyway, it's eleven am, and it takes twenty minutes to get there. My interview is at twelve and yours one-thirty, right?'

'Right.'

He grimaces. 'Hopefully the swelling on your lip will have gone down by then.'

I feel at my lip. Shit, it's all puffy. Fucking fabulous. Hopefully by the time I get there they'll have turned into Kylie Jenner lips. Miracles do happen, right?

'How the hell did we sleep in? We set the alarm.' I peer up at it and see it's flashing. It had definitely gone off. 'Goddamn it.' I sigh.

'What?'

I pick up the clock and turn up the radio volume until we can hear it. 'The volume was all the way down.' Some funny bastard obviously thought that would be hilarious.

'Well, come on. We need to shift arse.'

We get ready quickly, pack up all our stuff, pay for the room, and head to the car. Felix insists on carrying the luggage, so I grab his jacket from the bathroom and place it on the backseat, so it doesn't get creased. I keep mine on, which I regret after ten minutes of driving as it's a warm day and my air con is not the best. I feel sweat slick between my breasts. Lovely.

'I can't believe we didn't even have time to have the free coffee and biscuits from the room.' I groan. They're my favourite part about staying in a hotel.

'Oh, here.' He reaches down the side of the car and flings a wrapped biscuit at me. 'Breakfast.'

'My hero,' I fake gush. 'Can you unwrap it for me? Bit difficult while I'm driving.'

'God, you're such a Princess.'

I pull up at the school and we walk into the reception and give our names.

'You're very early Mr Montague.' The receptionist says.

'I know, but we travelled down together. I'll just hang around, it's not worth going anywhere else.'

We're directed to the waiting room and I nervously take a seat.

'You're like a jelly, woman. Good job you didn't have a coffee this morning.' Felix says, grabbing my shaking thigh to try to steady it.

'I know. I just need a job. Yesterday was a shambles. I've got to do better today.'

'Miss Cornish?'

'Good luck.' he tells me with a wink.

The headteacher, a Mr Smith, introduces himself and his fellow interviewer, another teacher called Mrs Ross. I reach out to shake their hands in turn. I'm shaking like a bloody leaf. Shit, I think I have hypoglycaemia from not eating enough. I do occasionally get it if I'm hungry.

Then I notice a side-eye pass between them and I remember my bruised mouth. I point to it. 'I fell out of bed this morning. Hit my mouth on the bedside table.'

'That must have been painful.' Mrs Ross says with concern.

'It was. Especially as I wasn't expecting it.'

'Well, I don't think anyone expects to fall out of bed, do they?' She smiles, clearly finding me amusing.

'It helps if the person you're sharing with knows you're there.' I ramble on. Please, God, get my nervous mouth to shut up. I always ramble when I'm nervous.

'Erm...' Mrs Ross looks at the papers on her desk.

'Let's start the interview, shall we?' Mr Smith interrupts.

I think the interview goes quite well and I'm hopeful I might be in a chance of getting the job. York is such a pretty place, I know I would enjoy living here. The only thing that's annoyed me is I've had to keep sitting to one side because of my bee sting. That and the fact I can't stop shaking. I really must get something to eat after this interview. I wonder if they'll allow me to eat in the school canteen?

The interview over, Mrs Ross tells me she'll escort me to the door.

Just outside she pulls me to one side. 'You don't have to be afraid. You can tell me if you're being abused.'

'Pardon?' I ask, completely startled. She thinks I'm being bloody abused?

She smiles kindly. 'You're shaking like a leaf. You have a swollen mouth. There's obviously some injury stopping you from sitting properly, and you said your other half didn't know you were in the bed. I'm guessing he makes you sleep on the floor. I had a friend like that once. She got help. Started a brand-new life. I guess he hit you, right? That's why you have the swollen lip. I can get you a number. Ring them.'

I grab her arm. 'No. Seriously. Felix did not hit me. I snuck into his bed in the early hours. He didn't know I was there.'

'You snuck into your partner's bed?' She questions. 'Don't you see how crazy that sounds. Most couples share.'

'We're just sharing a room. We're attending interviews together. It's a long story.'

She doesn't look convinced. 'Well, I'm here if

you need me, if you need someone to talk to. If you "accidentally" fall out of bed again.'

'Thank you, but seriously, I'm fine.'

We head back into the waiting room. 'Well, it was lovely to meet you, Katy.'

I smile back at her. 'Likewise. This is Felix Montague, by the way. We came together though his interview isn't until later.'

'Didn't trust you alone?' She questions.

I shake my head. 'Seriously, no. We're great friends. Aren't we, Felix?'

'Besties,' he says, before giving Mrs Ross one of his killer smiles. He receives a dead-eye in return.

'We'll be in touch,' says Mrs Ross before turning on her heel.

'What the fuck was that all about?' Felix questions.

'She thinks you beat me up. I had to tell her you didn't.'

'Fucking what? Katy, how can I go into the interview and face someone who thinks I'm a woman beater?' His eyes widen.

'I told her she had the wrong end of the stick. You'll be fine. Where's your jacket?' I ask him.

'Fuck, it's on the back seat of the car still. I'm just going to grab it.' He runs out of the school.

When he returns his face is a grim mask, 'What the hell did you do to my jacket, Katy?' His voice is a menacing rumble.

Mrs Ross appears, obviously catching him berating me. She stares at him like she wants to have him arrested there and then.

'Miss Drummond, would you like to come through?'

'I can explain,' Felix says, walking over to Mrs Ross and lifting his jacket up to her, opening it up. He places it under her nose, accidentally brushing her top lip with the jacket. She veers back, scared half to death by the thoughts of being attacked by a woman beater. 'She washed my jacket in strawberry body wash. I smell like a girl.' Felix whines.

He's not really helping his case here.

'Mr Montague. If you could kindly take your seat and wait for your own interview.' Mrs Ross' face is now taut as she attempts to keep her emotions in check. 'Miss Drummond, I apologise for the interruption, please come through.'

They leave the room and Felix stands up, 'Come on, let's get some lunch. There might be a Wetherspoons with a meal and beer for a fiver. I need it.'

'But your interview?' My brow furrows.

'What did you use to clean my jacket, Katy?' Felix questions.

'You know what, my strawberry body wash.'

'Yeah but how did you get the stain out?'

'I scrubbed it with my bath sponge, why?' This man gets weirder I swear.

'Because when Mrs Ross looked back up at me asking me to take a seat she had a pubic hair on the top of her lip.' He replies. 'So funnily enough, what with her thinking I'm into domestic violence too, I think I'll call this one quits. Now let's get that beer.'

He stalks out of the school and I have to run behind him to keep up. I wonder at what point in the interview someone is going to point out to poor Mrs Ross that she has a pube on her face? That poor woman, all she did was try to help me. If I had been a victim of domestic violence she would have done her best to assist me. I could tell.

Taking out my interview schedule from my handbag, I dial the schools number. I could go back in, we're only a few yards away, but I think that school has experienced enough already at the hands of me and Felix.

'Hi. I'm afraid that Mr Montague won't be attending his interview after all.' I tell the receptionist.

'Oh,' she replies back. 'I'm sorry to hear that. Listen, is Mr Montague single? Could you pass him my number...?'

I snap the phone shut. 'Unbelievable.' I shout out as I get behind the wheel again, winding the windows down as the car is like an oven. 'Fucking unbelievable.'

'What now?' Felix says. 'Can we just get to a spoons and get my beer? I can't cope with any more drama today.'

'The receptionist wants your number.' I shout out. 'The fact you're potentially violent doesn't seem to have put her off in the slightest.'

He reaches for me with his hand. I veer back.

'I was only going to tickle your cheek and say 'is Katy-waty jealous'." He rolls his eyes.

'Well, I don't want you near my lip. I need it to settle down before the next interview.' I sigh when I think about the journey. 'In Newquay. Just six and a half hours drive away.'

'Dear God,' says Felix, 'Six and a half hours stuck with you? I'll probably kick you out of the car halfway and leave you at the roadside.'

'That right, Sir? Would you like to step outside the car?' We turn around to find a policeman stood at the side of our vehicle, next to Felix. I notice that while we were engrossed in conversation a police car has pulled in behind us.

'We've had reports about your potential safety, Miss Cornish. Just need to ask a few questions.'

Felix's stomach rumbles and I shake as my hypoglycaemia worsens.

'No need to be scared, love. We're here to help.' The policeman places a hand on my arm in reassurance.

Oh dear.

# Chapter 9

### Katy

I wake up from my nightmare, my neck stiff from leaning awkwardly against the car door. Why have I been having that same dream recently? It's always I'm desperate for the loo and the only toilet I can find is in public. Like, a toilet right in the middle of a department store, kind of busy. Maybe it's because I got caught short the other day.

I look at my watch. Wow, I've slept most of the journey. I suppose having to persuade a police officer that Felix isn't a wife beater took it out of me.

'We're nearly there,' Felix says, tossing me a Mars bar.

I'm still too asleep to catch it, instead it smacks me on the boob before falling on my lap.

'Ouch! Boob attacker.'

He grins. 'I can't help it that all boobs are naturally drawn towards me.'

I scoff. 'You wish.' I push my arms up in the air and stretch out my muscles. I notice him shamelessly check out my tits. He really can't help himself. 'Bugger, I can't believe I slept so long.' I unwrap the bar and shove some in my mouth. I need the chocolate. Mmm, I let the sugar soothe me.

Then I notice he has a bag full of treats. A lot like how I'd normally treat myself when I'm due on my period. 'Remember we have to be tight with our budget?' I remind him.

He rolls his eyes. 'Yes, thank you, money saving expert.'

I hate how he's always making me out to be a huge stick in the mud.

'Hey, I'm being serious. I counted our money before I collapsed, and we only have one hundred and eight pounds left. Well, we did, before you went and bought every chocolate bar in the world.'

He shrugs. 'Okay, so maybe it's more a clear one hundred now. It's not the end of the world.'

'Shit, one hundred quid left and we're only on day two. We are so gonna run out of money. Then what will we do?'

'Don't you have any other savings?' he asks, as if this whole thing is no big deal.

'Nope. I used up my savings for mine and Dick's trip to Paris last month. Big waste of time that was.'

'Jesus, you paid for you guys to go to Paris?' he asks. I nod my head in answer. 'I suppose I shouldn't be surprised. The guy sounds like a right cock. But I assumed you'd have savings. Isn't that what sensible girls like you do?'

I balk. 'Excuse me? Sensible girls like me? Are you saying I'm boring?'

He snorts. 'Well, before this trip I would have definitely said that, but now I'm starting to find you slightly entertaining.'

'Gee, thanks. So I take it you don't have any other money?'

'Babe, the money I gave over is all the money to my name right now.'

Babe. I hate being called that. Especially by him in his southern drawl.

'Snap.' I look out the window. 'God, when did our lives become so shit?'

'Around the time a woman asked me to help with her break up.'

I grimace. This is kind of all my own fault. If I

could have just kept away from bloody Felix Montague we wouldn't be in this huge mess.

'Don't worry,' he reassures with a quick squeeze of my thigh. 'Soon we'll have a job and everything will be looking up.'

Just when I think he won't say a nice thing to me, he surprises me.

'Well, *I'll* have a job,' he clarifies. 'I'm not overly confident for you.' He winks to let me know he's joking. It's still pretty cheeky.

Ugh, and now I have to pee.

'Can we pull over? I really need a wee.'

'You and your bloody bladder. Can't you wait? I reckon we're only about fifteen minutes from the hotel.'

'I'm sorry, but I really can't.'

He huffs. 'Fine.' He pulls over into a public car park.

I look around at the dark sky, a sudden chill running down my spine. 'Would you...'

'What?' he snaps bad temperedly. I suppose he has just been driving for six hours.

'Would you... come with me?' I ask pathetically.

'Sorry, but you want me to hold your hand while you pee on the grass?'

'Yes, okay! It's dark out and it's not safe for a

woman like me to be getting her bits out for everyone to see.'

He rolls his eyes. 'Look around. There's no one here. And I can't see any bees around either.'

I glare at him. 'Please?'

'Ugh, fine.' He gets out of the car and follows me as I use the torch on my phone to find a secluded area by some bushes. 'Come on then. Get your vag out.'

I punch him in the stomach. He doesn't even flinch. Damn, that's a six pack right there. The glorious bastard.

'Just shut up, will you?'

'Come on, it's nothing I haven't seen before.'

I pull my trousers down, careful to hide myself from him the best I can, and then I squat, ready to do my business.

'Hello!' a voice booms from behind us. It catches me so off guard, my legs tremble and I find myself falling forward onto Felix's crotch.

'Agh!' he screams, like a little girl. 'Why the fuck would you head butt me in the nuts?'

'Didn't mean to interrupt,' the voice says again, shining a torch at us.

I think about how we must appear. Me on my knees, my trousers and knickers down my ankles, and Felix clutching his knob through his trousers. Jesus!

'Are you here for the festival?' the man asks. I can just about make out that he's about fifty and wearing rainbow tie-dye clothes. Bloody nosy hippy.

'No–'

Felix straightens himself out, quickly standing in front of me. 'Festival? Yes, we're here for the festival.' He looks back at me in warning. 'The only problem is that we've forgotten our tickets.'

'Ah, well that's alright. Stick with me and I'll get you in.'

'Okay great,' Felix smiles. 'Well, then lead the way.'

He strides off ahead of us. 'What the hell are you doing?' I hiss at Felix.

'Getting us into a free festival. You're welcome.'

"Don't go too far, I'll catch you up. I still need my wee." Felix shakes his head at me and walks off slowly in front following the guy. I quickly wee, then crossing my arms I run to catch him up begrudgingly. It's not like I'm going to sit in the car waiting on my own. We walk for what seems like miles.

'You realise this guy could be leading us to our deaths?' I whisper to Felix.

He cracks a smile. 'Where's your sense of adventure, Kitty Kat?'

God, he's annoying as fuck.

We eventually feel sand under our feet and hear the distant echoes of the waves. We're on a beach? Thank God I had my wee, the sound of water would have finished me off.

'Here it is,' the guy says pointing towards something that looks like a big bonfire in the distance.

I fasten my pace, eager to find out what we're heading for, but slow down when I feel Felix take my hand. I look at him, but he doesn't say anything, nor does he look at me. He just keeps walking.

It annoys me that I like the feel of my hand in his. I'm so weak.

When we get to crowds of people, everyone smiles at our friend and we have beers thrust into our hands.

'It's going to start soon,' he says, finding his way off. 'Have a great night.'

I turn to Felix, my hand still in his and raise my eyebrows. 'Well, what the hell are we doing here?'

'We're having an adventure, Kitty Kat. Try to live a little.'

I roll my eyes and down my beer. His eyes nearly pop out of their sockets.

'Whoo! Get you!'

I smile back, glad at his encouragement and approval. 'So what time do you think the music will start?'

He shrugs. 'No idea.'

Music suddenly blares out of speakers, except it's not the usual fast paced energetic beats you'd expect at a festival. Instead it's some kind of laid back melody.

'See,' Felix says smugly. 'There's the music.'

I get handed another beer by someone. 'Okay, I'll admit it. This is kind of fun.'

I mean, at least we get free beer.

'Told you.'

I smile around at the crowd. They all seem to be shuffling around to the music. Hang on a minute. Are they shuffling to the music or are they removing their clothes? Uh-oh. They're definitely removing their clothes. What the hell is going on here?

'Err... Felix?'

He takes my arm and pulls me closer. I look down at it, pleased at the small protection it offers me. I look back and men and women of all ages are now fully naked: tits, vag, arse, and dicks, on full display for everyone.

'Come on, you too,' the guy who brought us here says, suddenly at our side, completely bollock fucking naked.

'Oh, no thanks,' I say with a smile. 'I'm going to keep my clothes on for now.'

'She's a bit of a prude at first,' Felix says with a grin, removing his jacket and top. Jesus, why is he getting naked? Damn, look at that six pack! Why isn't he naked more often?

'Felix!' I snap just as a leggy blonde comes up to him and touches his chest. Jesus, her pubic hair is out of control. It's like a forest down there!

'Come on,' a sleazy guy with a moustache says, taking my hips and trying to force me to sway to the music. I freeze, my whole body shutting down. How the fuck can this be happening? Could this be a nightmare? Maybe I'm still safely asleep in the car?

'Hey!' Felix shouts from behind me, so loud and close to my ears that I flinch. 'Get off her. She's with me.'

Sleazy guy's hands immediately leave my hips. 'Sorry, fella. But what on earth are you doing coming to a swinging festival if you want to be selfish?'

'A what now?' I blurt out, my mouth hanging open in shock.

'A swinging festival,' he repeats. 'I thought you guys said you had tickets?'

'We did,' Felix nods, pulling me back to his chest. Mmm, it's warm. 'We just like the thrill of watching.' He bats off leggy blonde's hands as if to prove a point.

'Ah! Why didn't you say! You should go on over to the watchers tent. Here, I'll take you.'

He turns and starts walking. I'm ready to bolt it out of there, but Felix takes my hand and drags me along after him.

'What the hell are you doing?' I whisper hiss. 'I don't want to watch.'

'We need to keep this guy sweet. We don't want this huge crowd turning on us. It could get ugly.'

I look around at all the balls surrounding me. 'It already has.'

Sleazy guy introduces us to Ciara, a lady with a whip, and an eye mask surrounding the most piercing green eyes I've ever seen before. She smiles friendly. 'Right guys, if you'd like to come through to a booth.'

I gulp but follow her. We're sat into a small booth where we have a view of a stage where a couple are making out, him finger fucking her roughly. Luckily, we can't see the other watchers. God knows what they're doing. I dread to think.

'Enjoy your evening,' Ciara smiles, giving come fuck me eyes to Felix, before sauntering off.

'Right, let's get out of here,' I say as soon as she's out of earshot.

He makes himself comfortable on the seat. 'Well, now we're here we might as well watch a bit of the show.'

'Sorry? You want me to watch porn with you?'

He laughs. 'You don't have to watch it; if it really scares you. But I wouldn't mind watching some.'

'God, you're a dirty bastard.'

I turn begrudgingly towards the stage and force myself to watch as the guy takes her tit in his mouth and sucks, drawing out a moan from her. God, why is this hot to watch? I can't remember the last time I had sex that looked this good.

He moves his mouth down to her pussy and starts going down on her. My lady parts tingle. Dick never liked doing that. Did it suddenly get hot in here?'

'See,' Felix whispers in my ear seductively. 'You're enjoying it.'

I blush, hitting him on the shoulder. 'No, I am not. I'm just watching it to keep you happy.'

He smiles devilishly. 'What else would you do to make me happy?' He waggles his eyebrows suggestively.

My chest rises and falls erratically, my traitorous breath coming out in short spurts. I don't answer him. I can't. Instead my eyes roam greedily over his naked chest.

'Look at you,' he grins. 'You're turned on.'

'No, I'm not!' I protest, hiding my face from him.

'Yes, you are. You do enjoy watching. You're all flushed, and you keep squeezing your thighs together.'

'I do not.'

'If you say so. Look, I'm turned on.' He points down at his erect dick straining against the fabric of his trousers. Jesus!

'Wow. You're not shy, are you?' I snort.

I turn away from him and focus on the couple on stage. He's fucking her now, his thrusts so relentless that she's moving up along the bed. Her face becomes flushed and then she's screaming in pleasure. Fuck.

I look back to Felix, who is no longer touching his dick. 'Shall we go then?'

'After you, pervert.'

---

We check in at reception, a new awkward atmosphere having settled over us. We didn't speak all the way to the car and the journey was even more intense. Felix collects the key to our room and we walk up the stairs.

I still can't get the images of that hot sex out of my head. That and Felix's dick. As we let ourselves in, I'm suddenly sure of what I need to do in order to sleep. I need to bash one out. But how the hell am I going to do that with Felix here?

'I'm just going to the loo,' he says.

Dammit. He took my idea. Unless I could do it while he's in there.

'Okay. How long do you think you'll be?'

He frowns at me. 'Sorry, are you asking if I'm taking a shit?'

'No! I just... wondered.'

'Well if I'm being completely honest, I plan to masturbate so I'll be a little while.'

My mouth drops open. 'Jesus, Felix! You really don't give a shit, do you?'

'Why be embarrassed?' he shrugs. I squirm,

eying the bed. 'Wait a minute. Why do you want to know?' He narrows his eyes at me. 'You want to touch yourself too, don't you?'

I blush scarlet. 'Shut up! Why is it funny when I do, but it's all natural when you want to?'

'It's not. I'm just shocked is all. God, Katy you're full of surprises.'

I start getting changed, hiding myself under the duvet. 'So could you wait until I tell you to come back in?'

He rolls his eyes. 'Look, we both know what we're doing. Why don't we just get into bed, turn our backs to each other and get on with it?'

'Excuse me?'

'At least that way we'll be comfortable.'

Oh my God. I can't masturbate with him in the same bed as me. Can I?

'But... what if I make a noise?'

'I personally think that would be fucking fantastic. If anything's going to get me off quicker, it's that. Unless the real question is if you'd like a hand?'

'You are one dirty bastard.'

'Change the record, Cornish. Let's just do this.'

I nod, turn away from him, and strip down to just my bra and knickers. Then I dive under the covers.

Are we really going to do this?

*C'mon, Katy. You wanted to live a little and hearing him will be a huge turn on.*

I close my eyes and imagine watching the couple again. Sliding a hand over the top of my knickers, I just leave it there, feeling my heat. I really don't think I can go through with this.

Then I hear a slapping type noise coming from behind me and faster breathing.

Oh my God. He's wanking behind me. That man doesn't give a shit. He's straight at it!

"C'mon, Katy. I'm lonely on my own," he taunts.

The way he says it makes my juices run; it's like he's actually talking to me *during sex*, like as if we're doing it. Well, I'm not being left out.

I slip my fingers under the leg of one side of my panties and rub them through my slickness. Oh, fuck this, I'm taking them off. I wriggle out of them and toss them out of bed and then take off my bra and do the same. I feel liberated. Now I can grab my own tits and squeeze them in just the way I like, not doing what Dick used to do and pinch my nipple like he was pegging me out on the washing line.

STOP THINKING ABOUT DICK!

Well, not THAT Dick.

Closing my eyes, I focus in on the sounds that Felix is making, those weird slapping noises. I decide

I'm going to go all porn star on his arse and see if it turns him on. I touch myself, writhing under my own fingers and begin to moan.

'Ohhhhh.'

I cup a breast in my hand and bite my bottom lip. 'Oh God yes, yes.'

Felix's slaps get faster, and he starts making a noise, 'Unnn, unn, unnn.'

It's working! My words are turning him on. I let myself get a bit louder. To be honest I'm fucking well turning myself on. I plunge two fingers of one hand into my wetness and tickle my clit with a finger of my other hand. With my movements and my ears focused on the sound of Felix grunting my body craves its orgasm.

"Oh yeah, oh yeah, baby. Just there, right there. Fuck me, oh please, fuck me."

Slapslapslapslapslapslapslap

'Unnnunnnnunnnnnunnnnunnnnunnn'

'Uunnnphhh, haaaaahhhhhhhh.'

His voice and noises take me over the edge and wave after wave comes over me as I explode, my pussy contracting around my fingers.

I push my face into the pillow, waiting until my breathing starts to return to normal. And then I feel my face go beet red. Shit! I just fingered myself back to back with Felix in the same bed.

I open my eyes and realise that actually I've moved. Totally carried away with what I was doing I've moved onto my back and Felix is now turned towards me, his spent cock in his hand, grinning at me like a loon.

"Better?" He asks.

"Fantastic." I reply smiling back, glad the duvet is covering my naked body.

"Well, I'm just going to the bathroom to clean up."

"Okay."

When he's gone I quickly wipe myself down with my discarded pants and once again fling them on the floor and then I close my eyes and make fake sleeping noises for when Felix returns.

# Chapter 10

### Katy

I wake up to find him already awake and staring at me. I quickly cover my face with the duvet.

'Why are you staring at me?' I grunt. We might have masturbated together last night but this morning all of my regular awkward feelings for him are back. I can't believe I did that in front of him. I can't even blame the alcohol.

He grins. 'Just watching you dribble and wondering when you were going to wake up. I didn't want to start banging around and wake you up in a terrible mood.'

'Oh. That's very thoughtful of you.'

'I'm a very thoughtful guy. You should know that by now.'

I roll my eyes. 'Whatever. I suppose I can really get to know you once we get to your parents' house tonight. See all of your embarrassing family photos.'

His face drops. 'They might have raised me, but that doesn't mean they know me, Katy.'

'Do you not get on with them?'

He sighs. 'It's a long story.'

'O...kay. Anyway, let's get ready.'

---

After an awkward breakfast on my part—he clearly has no shame—we're waiting in reception of St Saviours school. It looks pretty posh here. Yet, instead of a regular interview we're having an informal workshop. I hate these things. They say they're informal, but they're always judging you, following you around like a creepy psychologist watching animals in a zoo.

'Good morning, everyone,' a lady says, walking into the room dressed in a tight navy pencil skirt and sharp white shirt.

Oh my God. Why does she seem familiar?

'Fuck,' I hear Felix gasp.

'What is it?' I whisper at him.

'It's the Domme from last night.'

My eyes widen. I turn back to look at her. The Domme? I look at her face, and although last night it was partly obscured by a mask, I can still make out it's the woman that showed us to our 'watching booth'. I'd recognise those piercing green eyes anywhere. Oh my God. How the hell can this woman be running this workshop?

'Today I'd like you to get into pairs and await further instruction.'

Felix bumps me on the shoulder. 'Better the devil you know.'

I smile faintly back. 'Do you think she recognises us?'

'We'll soon find out.'

'You two.' I look up to see that she's pointing at us. 'If you could come centre stage please.'

I bet she's used to stages, dirty bitch. I try to work out if she's recognised us and plans on humiliating us, but she has a poker face.

Felix nudges me forward. I attempt to snap myself out of it and walk into the middle of the circle of people, feeling like I'm about to be eaten by lions.

'Now,' she continues. 'I want you to imagine yourself as an animal. Don't tell us, or your partner what you are.'

An animal? Shit. Okay, think, think. Panda. That's the only animal I can think of right now.

'I want you to act out your animal to your partner, without making any noise.'

'So, sort of like charades?' Felix checks.

'Exactly,' she nods. 'You just sit back and *watch*.'

Wait a second, was that a reference to us watching last night?

I can feel the back of my neck sweating. I pull my hair back with my emergency hair scrunchie. Right, how the hell do I act like a panda?

What the hell do I know about them? I've only ever saw them plodding around in zoo's eating bamboo. That's it! I'll eat bamboo!

So I pretend to yank a piece of a tree, wrapping my hand around it and bringing it to my mouth. I pretend to bite and chew, before repeating the whole thing again. Felix looks at me with raised eyebrows, a confused expression on his face. Jesus, why did I have to pick something so difficult? But I've committed now.

'Start guessing, Felix,' the lady instructs.

'Err... a bear?'

I shake my head.

'Try describing what she's doing,' she says forcibly.

I can tell he's starting to panic now too, although he's trying to cover it with a bemused mask.

'Umm... well, if anything, it looks like she's giving the world's worst blow job.'

Silence descends upon the room. Did he seriously just say that?

The lady's eyebrows raise. 'Is he close?' she asks me with amusement.

'I'm a panda!' I shout. 'A fucking panda! Why the hell would you think of a blow job?'

'Sorry,' he grimaces. 'But come on, what the hell were you doing?'

'I was eating bamboo, you idiot.'

'Okay,' the woman claps, obviously bored of our little shit show. 'This exercise was to see how intuitive you are and how you can work as a team. I'm assuming you two know each other; which is strange as you don't seem to be intuitive to each other at all.'

I glare at him. Well, he's fucked this up for us.

We have to sit through everyone else doing stupid animal impressions. They all obviously go for far easier animals like cats and dogs. Why didn't I think to be a dog? Or a cat, licking themselves? It would have been easy. Although knowing Felix, he'd have shouted out something ridiculous like 'vagina licking!' What is wrong with that bloody man!

'Well, that was a complete waste of time,' I whinge once we're in the car. 'And we only have one hundred quid left. I was kind of hoping I'd have been offered a job by now.'

'The competition is tough though,' he says with a wink.

'Why on earth would you shout out blow job? I mean, of all the things to say in a job interview.'

'Don't make out it wasn't in reference to what you were doing. You should have seen yourself.' He doubles over laughing.

'Ha ha, very funny. Just let it be noted that you screwed this up for us.'

'It was fucked from the minute that woman walked in. Are you honestly telling me she'd consider hiring two people who she'd seen the night before at a sex show?'

I cringe. 'God, I still can't believe we went.'

'Well, brace yourself. If you think that was shocking, wait 'til you meet my parents.'

# ROAD TRIP

We pull up outside a semi, situated on a busy main road, after yet another long-arsed drive. I look up at the red peeling front door, at the overgrown bushes crowding around the windows. It's not the homeliest looking place in the world.

'You ready for my parents?' he asks, carrying our bags to the front door.

'What, do they have three heads or something?'

He scoffs. 'I wish it was that explainable. They're just... shall we say, set in their ways?'

He lets himself in and I follow him through to the sitting room.

'Hello?' he calls.

'Hiya, love,' a blonde lady in her fifties says from the sofa. 'We weren't expecting you 'til later.' She stands up, cigarette still in her hand, to hug him. Then she turns her attention on me. 'And you must be his lady friend, Catherine.'

'Oh hi, but it's just Katy.'

'Don't sell yourself short with a nickname, my darlin'. Look at the Duchess of Cambridge. She used to go by Kate, but now she's gone back to Catherine. Far more regal, if you ask me.'

Felix rolls his eyes. 'Mum loves the royal family,' he explains.

'Who bloody doesn't! Am I right?' She laughs. 'Am I right, Catherine?'

I laugh. 'But seriously, I was christened Katy.'

She reacts in horror as if I've slapped her. 'Sorry? You were christened Katy? Why on earth would your mother do that to you?'

'Er... I don't know,' I shrug. 'Just liked it, I guess.'

'What's your siblings names?' she asks in amusement.

'My sister is called Victoria.'

'There we go! A real regal name right there. I wonder why your mum decided to give you such a common name next to her. How strange.'

'Mum!' Felix says, 'stop will you. Katy is our guest.'

'She knows I'm only joking, don't you love?' She smiles like we're both in on some inside joke.

'Of course,' I smile.

'Where's Dad anyway?'

The front door suddenly slams. 'Ah, here he is.'

A portly man that Felix looks a lot like, comes walking in cursing to himself.

'Oh, hi mate,' he says to Felix, giving him an awkward pat on the back.

'You alright, Dad?'

'Ah, just having trouble with those bloody

Eastern Europeans again.' He rolls his eyes.

'Sorry?' I ask. Is his Dad some kind of racist or something?

'Mainly the Polish around here,' his Dad confirms. 'Bringing this bloody area down with their Polish markets. It's a disgrace if you ask me. I'm glad we're having Brexit. I just wish they'd ship the lot of them back.'

Wow. So his Dad *is* a racist.

'Anyway, Dad, it's getting late. We're gonna head up to bed.'

'You must be hungry,' his mum says. 'I'm sure Katy here would like some food.'

I grin eagerly. 'Yes please.' Right now, I'm so hungry I don't care if I have to listen to more racist rants. Just put food in my belly.

The meal is fairly pleasant. I feel sorry for Felix who keeps cringing every time his parents say something embarrassing. Which is kind of every single sentence that leaves their mouths.

His parents hug us goodnight before we make our way upstairs.

'Sorry about them,' he says, with a sad smile.

'Hey, they're your parents. Nothing to apologise for. We can't choose them.' I smile back at him in what I hope is a reassuring manner.

## Chapter 11

### Felix

Waking up in my old bed feels weird enough, but to look over and see Katy in just her knickers and bra squeezing herself into a pencil skirt... well, it's enough to give me a bad case of morning wood. When she turns around, I quickly close my eyes, feigning sleep. It's easier than admitting she turns me on.

She leaves the room. God, why is she getting breakfast so early? She told me last night that the interview had been pushed back to two pm. It's only nine am. Unless... no, she wouldn't. Would she? She wouldn't have lied about the time so that I'd miss it? Right?

## Katy

The stupid bastard believed me when I told him the interview had been moved to the afternoon. He's going to miss it and that'll mean more chance of me getting hired. Whenever he's around, there's nothing but trouble and as I laid in bed last night, I gave myself a pep talk. I can't let myself get distracted by his pretty face and even worse than that, I can't start liking this guy. He's my competition.

I hurry into the car and pull out of the drive. The front door opens and out runs Felix, pulling up trousers; a white shirt on his shoulders but undone. He spots me, and his face turns murderous. He runs at the car, launching himself onto the bonnet.

'What the hell are you doing?' I scream.

'I'm not going to miss this interview!' he shouts, clearly already onto me.

'Oh yes you are.' I put the car into drive, picking up a speed of twenty before screeching on the brakes. He flies from it. Shit. Is he okay? I hope I haven't killed the guy.

He jumps up as quickly as he went down. Crap. I floor the accelerator, leaving him standing there. Looking back in my rearview mirror, I cackle as he stands in the road, his face red with fury.

I look back at the road just in time for me to see the traffic at a halt. I slam the brakes on to avoid crashing into the back of a Ford Fiesta. Shit. That's the last thing I need, a car crash.

Why the hell is there so much traffic? This is going to make me late.

Felix slams his hands against my window, his smug smile taking over his face. 'Ha ha!' he taunts before running off ahead, missing the traffic. Crap. He's going to beat me and no doubt once he gets there he'll start bad-mouthing me. I toot my horn, but there's nothing I can do. Something serious must have happened to get this sort of standstill.

He's about two hundred yards in front of me now. Oh, fuck it. I pull my car over onto the curb, put the hazards on and jump out. If he can run it, then so can I.

I sprint towards him, narrowly missing a cyclist. The cocky bastard has slowed his pace now, so sure I'm still stuck in traffic. I laugh as I run past him, all of my previous cross-country experience helping me along. I might have been fifteen at the time, but I've still got it.

His mouth drops before he's running next to me. He has the bare arsed cheek to shove me to the right. I stumble, so shocked he'd hurt a woman, to give him a chance to overtake me. I growl. This means war.

I pass someone selling fresh baked French sticks. Grabbing one without paying, the man shouts abuse after me and I chase up to Felix. I smack him hard over the head with it. He trips, clutching at his head, stumbling down onto his knees.

'Ha ha!' I laugh, running ahead.

I turn the corner and run into Japanese tourists that are clearly lost. Why the hell would you visit Harrow? I bat them out of the way, Harrow school in my vision. Once I get there I can straighten myself out.

Something hits me in the centre of my back, temporarily winding me. I turn to see Felix running behind me lobbing apples at me. There's a greengrocer running after him shouting about him being a thief.

I fight against the stitch in my stomach and run through it, apples hitting me on the arms. Who knew they'd hurt so bad?

'Stop cheating, you bastard!' I scream back at him.

He grabs my hair and pulls until I'm level paced with him. I push him into a pile of rubbish bags. He goes down like a sack of potatoes. Ha!

He stumbles out and catches up to me in a second. He pushes me into a couple sitting outside a café. I fall onto the table, their coffees spilling and scalding my hand. Agh, that hurts like a motherfucker!

I'm going to kill him.

I grab the cup and run after him, lobbing it at his head. It hits him right on the ear.

'Fuck!' I hear him hiss.

The doors to the school are in sight now and we're at an even pacing. He keeps trying to push me away, but I shove him right back.

We both squeeze through the door and rush to the receptionist.

'I'm here,' I wheeze, out of breath, 'for the interview.'

The receptionist looks over us in disgust. If I look half as sweaty as I feel I can understand why. I look over Felix. His shirt still only has two buttons done up; it hangs loosely over his trousers. His back is damp against the shirt as is his forehead which glistens against the sunlight. How is it he still looks hot? It's beyond annoying.

'So, you're Katy Cornish?'

'Yes,' I nod eagerly, attempting to straighten my hair down.

'And I'm Felix Montague.'

'Okay,' she nods. 'We're tight on time today so we're going to interview you together. I hope that's okay with you.'

Oh dear.

'Fine by me,' Felix taunts, looking at me with raised eyebrows, 'Is that fine with you Miss Cornish?'

I smile through gritted teeth. 'Fine by me, Mr Montague.'

'Would you like some drinks?'

We both ask for a water and then are led to the interview room, Felix frantically doing up his shirt buttons. We're sat down with our iced waters and told the headmistress won't be long. As soon as the door's shut I'm pulling my pocket mirror out and looking at the mess of myself.

'You look hot,' he jokes. 'As in a hot mess.'

I clench my jaw, refusing to bother with a witty comeback. He doesn't deserve my response right now.

'In fact,' he continues, 'you look really hot. Here, let me cool you down.' He grabs the ice out of his drink, yanks my trousers to the side and throws them down my knickers.

Ice so cold polar bears in the arctic would be forced to shiver, slides onto my lady parts, so cold I physically shiver. I open my mouth to let out a scream in an attempt to alleviate some of the discomfort but at that exact moment the headmistress walks in.

'Hello, sorry to have kept you.'

'Not a bother,' Felix says, as smooth as caramel. The bastard. 'Me and Katy here are old friends anyway.'

'Oh lovely,' she coos, looking at me.

I try with every fibre of my body to appear normal, not like I'm living this agony and wanting nothing more than to stand up and shake until it goes down my leg. But I can't do that. I'd look like a dog shaking itself after a piss.

I force a smile though I'm sure my lips must be blue right now with the way she's looking back at me. With wide, amused eyes.

'You'll have to excuse Miss Cornish,' Felix says, 'but she suffers a bit with social anxiety.'

I cannot believe him.

'I'm fine,' I insist, leaning over on my right arse cheek to try to move the melting ice cube. To my absolute horror, icy water starts running down my leg, pooling loudly onto the floor.

Everyone hears it. The woman's eyes look like they're going to burst out of her head.

'She also has a problem with incontinence,' Felix says, with a hand on my shoulder.

---

I storm out of the school, leaving a trail of dripping water in my wake. He's done it again! We're never going to get a fucking job at this rate. In fact, we'll be placed on a banned list if we're not careful.

We have a hundred pounds to our name. Time to get a job is running out and I'm starting to get worried. Although right now I'm too angry to be anxious.

"Now what are we going to do?" I yell.

"Look, let me go back in there and explain, and see if they'll interview us again." Felix says.

"Okay." I sigh. "Well, be quick."

He isn't quick. He's gone for twenty minutes. In the meantime, my temper has built to astronomical proportions.

He finally reappears.

"Well?"

"Sorry, they made me wait ages and then said no. I tried."

"After all this time in the cold, I've probably got chapped lips." I snarl, "and nothing a Chapstick is going to do anything for." I begin to storm down the drive.

"Slow down, Kitty Kat. We ran here. I've not got the energy to run back to the car."

"Screw you." I flip him the middle finger as I carry on power walking.

"Oh, is that an offer? I'll hurry up for that." He quips.

I stand still, glaring at him. If my parts weren't already frozen from the cube attack, I might have the energy to attack him. Is there a hot water bottle for vaginas? I bet one of those handheld ones would work, thaw my poor tuppence out.

I begin walking again, though at a slower pace as my legs are starting to ache. Spying the flower bed display sign near where I left the car, I stare but the car isn't there. Oh, they must have sponsored more than one flower bed, makes sense. We'll just have to keep on walking. Although I felt sure it was just here, I remember knocking that gerberas head off.

"Felix?"

"Talking to me now, are you?"

"The car's gone."

Felix stares at the flowerbed and starts walking around.

"It's not hidden under a pile of poppies, you

dickhead." I shout. "Someone's stolen my car." I screech. "Phone the police."

After telling me to calm myself down and making me sit on the grass, Felix calls the police where he finds out that actually my car has been impounded for being parked illegally. Great, just great.

We're given the address of where to collect it from and get a taxi there as we've no idea what buses run there. That costs us a tenner and then we're charged ninety quid to get my car released. NINETY QUID. Leaving our combined funds as ZERO.

"We have no money, Felix. I'm already putting petrol on my credit card with no idea of how I'm going to pay it. I'm not getting any further in debt. What are we going to do?"

"We're going to pack and leave, get in the car and start the unbearably boring, long drive to Scarborough. It's almost half-eleven, so we can go back to Mum's and raid the fridge. Stuff our faces and then get in the car and on our way."

"Where are we going to stay, Felix?" I feel completely flat, like there's no point to this shit anymore.

"We'll figure something out. For now, let's make the most of the fact we have food and drink."

We head back to his house where his mum makes us a lunch spread and leaves us to it. There are sandwiches, crisps, chocolate biscuits, and tea. You've got to hand it to her, the woman might be a racist, but she sure knows how to put on a spread.

'Your mum is such a star,' I say, stuffing a sandwich in my mouth. I sound depressed even to my own ears.

'Come on, cheer up, Kitty Kat.'

I sigh. "Maybe a Dairylea Dunker might just make me feel a little better."

I grab one, stuffing it in my mouth. We eat in companionable silence. I really enjoy the taste of a tuna sandwich and let out a satisfied moan. Unfortunately, it sounds very similar to one of the sex noises I made the other night while bringing myself to climax.

"You okay there?" Felix says, a smirk appearing on his face.

I feel my cheeks heat. "Just enjoying my food."

"Ah, that's your enjoying yourself moan. Of course." He winks at me, "making a mental note."

"Stop it, Felix, please. I'm not in the mood. Not after the day we've had. We've not got yet another job and we've no money. I can't be cheery Katy all the time. I'm fucked off, and to be honest I'm thinking about just driving home."

'Katy.' Felix smiles kindly, his forehead wrinkled in concern. 'You have nowhere to live back home,' he reminds me softly.

Oh yeah. He's right. My parents will have moved by now. I'm basically an orphan.

'Besides, teaching is what you love. We need to carry on and do the rest of the interviews. Let's promise to behave and go to the interviews as professional as possible. If one of us gets a job, maybe we could help the other out until they do? We've spent all this time together, we could flatshare or something, if it comes to it?'

How can he be so sweet sometimes, when the rest of the time he acts like a total plank?

'Thank you.' I answer.

'You're welcome. See, things aren't that bad.'

'No, thank you for showing me that if I don't get a job, my option will be having to spend even more time with you. I'm totally getting this next job.'

'Well, thanks, mate.' Felix turns away in a huff. 'I thought we were friends.'

'Friends don't put ice cubes down their friend's pants.'

'Well, friends don't try to drive off to an interview without their friend and then get their car impounded and lose all their money.'

I sit with my head in my hands and start to sob. Once I start I just can't stop. Proper wailing, snot running down my nose, hysterical crying.

'I'm fucked. My life is ruined. My sister has won. She has everything, I have nothing. I'm a joke.'

Felix rushes over to me and lifts up my chin with his hand. 'Look at me.'

I look and sniffle. I can tell my eyes are puffy, they feel five times their normal size when I wipe my tears.

'Your sister has not won. She has your reject. You know he's an idiot and you're better off without him.'

I sniff.

He gets up, goes to the bathroom and returns, handing me a pile of toilet paper. 'Now clean up because green bogeys make me squeamish and you have a huge one on your top lip. Then let's get out of here. The sooner we're at Scarborough, the sooner we can prep for the next interview.'

I hastily wipe and blow my nose. How glamorous I am.

'But how are we going to prepare and look

professional when we're going to have to sleep in the car? How will we iron our suits?'

Felix goes in his pocket and draws out three twenty-pound notes.

'My mum gave me an emergency handout last night.'

I sit there stunned for a minute before I find my voice, and my temper.

'You let me get all upset and you had money all along? You're sick, do you know that? Sick. I bloody hate you.'

And with that I run to the bathroom to clean myself up and then get packed and head to the car. Felix follows along silently and clambers into the passenger side as I start the engine.

---

## Felix

I'm a shit. A total shit. Because I went back inside the Harrow school and begged them to interview me —and they did. And I can't tell Katy that right now because this, whatever it is, would all be over—and I don't want it to be.

Being back in my hometown reminded me how

much I love it. I knew I could connect with all of my old mates again. Plus, my parents aren't getting any younger and no matter how much they drive me insane, I would like to be closer to them.

So, I really wanted that job. It's possible I told the interviewers that I'd had to rush because I'd been assisting Katy who had medical issues and that's why I looked so hot and harassed and well, they said it showed what type of person I was that I'd abandoned the interview to look after her when she'd had the incontinence problem. They offered me the job on the spot and I accepted.

I. AM. A. TOTAL. SHIT.

I watch Katy now as she's driving. Her pretty face staring at the road straight ahead, her lips in a pout. She's not spoken to me for thirty minutes. Instead she put her CD on loud and has subjected me to Taylor Swift for the last half hour, with *Shake it Off* repeated several times.

'Please talk to me, Catherine.'

'No. And don't call me that, only your mother calls me that.'

'You just talked to me. Yeeasss, Kitty Kat is talking to me again!'

'God, you are so annoying.' She says.

'Look. I didn't want to tell you about my mum's

money because I'd decided that if we managed on our budget then we'd have a slap-up meal on the final evening, but then you got all girly emotional and so I thought I'd better fess up. Plus, we were penniless. So, no posh dinner but at least we can get a hotel for the night and even better there's an offer on the budget hotel, £29 a night.'

'Oh good, and so then we'll have thirty quid left.' She says.

'Yeah, about that... after tomorrow, we've no more interviews until Monday in Skegness, so how about we book two nights in the budget hotel and enjoy the seaside a bit? We've still got some food from my mum's.'

'What are we going to do Saturday? Where are we going to stay?'

I shrug my shoulders, although she doesn't see it as she's driving. 'Let's worry about Saturday on Saturday and just enjoy the next two days. There's no point us being miserable and what-iffing. We know if it comes to it we'll have to sleep in the car for a night. After Scarborough, I have a uni friend who lives in Newcastle, so I might give them a call.'

She lets out a huge exhale.

'Okay. You're right. And I love the seaside. Two

days in Scarborough it is. Unless I get a job and then you're on your own.'

When she says things like that I don't even want a job.

The other night when she was making herself come and she forgot herself, I saw a whole new side to her. I'd felt her move and so I'd looked over my shoulder and seen her laid on her back. The outside light shone on her body, one hand caressing a pert tit and then she'd gone to town down below.

Completely unbeknown to her I'd turned around, fisting my cock in my hand as I watched her bring herself off. I'd closed my eyes and imagined that I'd come all over those pert tits and then I'd waited, clutching my dick as she finished, my mind jealous of it being her own fingers inside herself instead of me.

I'd had to rush into the bathroom, and after cleaning up, splash my face with cold water. When I returned, and she was pretending to be asleep, it made me smile. She'd found a bit of confidence in herself and was trying to hide it again.

I like Katy for herself, but I know that she needs to gain more confidence, that by doing so she could have a great life. Only now my stupid body and brain have decided they want to be in that great life. In fact, right now I have a raging boner. I'm glad her eyes are on the road.

If Katy fails to get a job, I'll offer her a flat or house share with me in Harrow. But for now, I'll keep everything to myself. I don't want to think what will happen if she gets a job in another area and she'll be gone for good.

After two and a quarter hours driving, Katy pulls in at the edge of a petrol station.

'It's your turn to drive the rest of the way,' she tells me.

Oh, I like it when she gets all dominant.

## Chapter 12

### Katy

After driving for over two hours it's been lovely to close my eyes while Felix takes over. This morning has just been a tipping point for me. I've had enough of everything. But Felix was right—we don't know what's going to happen on Saturday but we're okay for the next day or so and that needs to be enough for now.

*Fly by the seat of your pants girl.* I tell myself. *Let yourself have some fun.*

We walk into the budget hotel and Felix goes about booking us in for two nights. I'm tired and hungry by this stage and can't wait to stretch my legs out and have a cuppa.

'You so owe me,' Felix says as he walks over with our room key, a beaming smile across his face.

'Why?' I ask.

'I got us an upgrade, Kitty Kat.'

My jaw drops. 'How did you manage that?'

'Well, they didn't have any budget rooms left so I put on my best doe-eyed expression, said we needed two nights and our budget was extremely limited and with you being pregnant and the hellish day we'd had this was the icing on the cake. The receptionist took one look at you, said "Oh wow, she does look pale and tired, I remember that stage well", and booked us into a bigger room for the £29 a night.'

I don't even care about the diss to my appearance. I've come to accept it from him now. Upgraded room whoo hoo.

'So what do we get extra?' I ask.

'I don't know. Let's go find out.'

Following him, I feel eyes staring at me from behind the reception desk. I give the receptionist a friendly wave and she nods at me like she's every sympathy for my plight. Fake exhaustion isn't required because I am. I add in a belly rub for good measure. I'm so going to hell.

When Felix opens the door, I almost manage the energy required to jump for joy. The room has a king-sized bed, a separate seating area, and as I look on the desk there is a complimentary small bottle of wine, two bottles of water and two packets of kettle chips!

There's also a note stating that two towelling robes are hanging in the wardrobe. I immediately shrug off my coat and pull mine out and wrap it around myself before cleaning a glass in the bathroom (has to be done), pouring half the bottle into my glass, grabbing the kettle chips and climbing inside the bed.

'That you done for the night is it?' Laughs Felix.

'It's certainly me done for the next few minutes.' I reply. 'Come join me.'

He quirks an eyebrow but follows suit though he doesn't wash his glass out. Boys are so dirty. With it being a king, he could lay right at the other side, but he doesn't, he scoots right up next to me.

'I'll raid my mum's bags next and see what else we can have for our in bed picnic.'

'Yaaayyy.' I clap my hands together, spreading crisp dust everywhere. 'This is gonna be so much fun.' I grab the remote off the bedside table and find a repeat of Tipping Point.

Felix rummages in the carrier bags his mother gave him and emerges with another bottle of wine, a tin of chocolate biscuits like you get given at Christmas, a packet of Cheesy Wotsits each and some breadcakes. We make crisp sandwiches. He shows me an apple, but I shake my head. Healthy eating can come later. For now, I'm enjoying myself.

'Think of the baby,' he jokes.

'So tell me more about yourself.' Felix suddenly says out of nowhere.

I raise my eyebrows. What is he trying to find out about me?

'I know you don't get along with your sister, but I want to learn more about you. What do you like and dislike? That kind of thing.'

I feel my cheeks flush from the sudden attention.

'I think you already know me a lot better than Dick ever did.'

He meets my gaze, his eyes full of something I can't put my finger on.

'Okay, let me think.' I tell him, desperately trying to think of something interesting to tell him about myself. 'Let's see. I like having really lazy days and eating junk food, so this right now is right up my street.' I stuff another chocolate biscuit in my mouth and don't say anything else until I've finished eating.

'I'm quite sensitive. You know like if you hear

people sniggering on a bus, and I'll think it must be about me. I realise I'm not very confident because I was prepared to settle for Richard as a boyfriend and husband, and well, now I seem to be having some sort of epiphany or mid-twenties crisis as I feel like I want to reach for more.'

He smiles kindly. 'You're just starting to value yourself. I wish you could see yourself like I see you.'

Why the heck is he suddenly being so nice to me? It's like we're on some kind of weird date. But then, any date where I get to sit in a dressing gown and eat crisps is a win for me.

'Why, how do you see me?' I ask, intrigued.

He looks over my face. I don't doubt I have crisp crumbs around my mouth.

'I see a beautiful, intelligent woman with a ton of career potential who just needs to believe in herself a bit more.'

I almost choke on another biscuit. Yes, it's my fourth. I'm having a picnic here, leave me alone.

'Oh, well, thank you.' I eventually say, unsure of what to say to that.

'You're welcome. Now, what are we doing this evening? We can carry on drinking here and just crash out, or we could head down to the seafront and

have a look around? We've two pounds left to spend.'
He laughs and I stare at him a bit too long cos I'm
kind of crushing on that beautiful face of his in my
inebriated state.

What if I just leant forward and kissed him?

What indeed? I do a strange flop face down on
the bed and crush the remaining food.

'Whoa, you a bit drunk there, missy?' Felix lifts
me up and I try to focus on which one is his face.
Whoa, how have I got so drunk? 'Right. I'm making
you a coffee and we'll just hang here for a bit longer
until you sober up.'

'You have a beautiful face and soul.' I tell him.

'Fucking hell you ARE pissed.' He says, with
wide eyes. 'A compliment.'

I lay back against the headboard, just feeling
mellow and entirely awesome, while I drink my
coffee.

'You take care of me so well, my beautiful friend.'
I tell him with a giggle. 'If you need me to take care of
you anytime, I will do.' Then I begin to giggle harder.
'Oh that sounds rude. No, I don't need to take care of
you in THAT way. I know now you can handle that
by yourself. Handle that, hand. You get it?' I crease
up laughing.

Felix chuckles, amusement dancing in his eyes as

he pushes a stray bit of hair out of my eyes. 'Yes, Kitty Kat.'

I sigh. 'I love you calling me Kitty Kat.'

My eyelids are suddenly so heavy, it's hard to keep them open, a fresh bout of fatigue taking over me. I let them close and allow sleep to take me.

---

I must have fallen asleep because the next time I open my eyes, Felix is sitting in the lounge chair reading the Scarborough magazine from the coffee table.

'What time is it?' I ask, pushing my hair out of my face. I move my hand and feel the dried saliva at the edge of my mouth. Sexy.

'Eight. You've not been asleep that long, maybe forty-five minutes or so.'

I still feel a bit merry, I think. Excellent, nice and buzzed.

'So can we go out now?' I ask, jumping out of bed to go to the bathroom. I stumble slightly. Okay, must move slower.

'Sure,' he shouts back. 'Just wash the dribble from your face and we're ready to go.'

We wander around the seafront. The smell of fish and chips is amazing, and we pay a pound of what we have left to buy a small cone to share. As we wander further up the street we walk past a face painter drawing a tiger face on a young boy who looks about five. Bit late for him to be out.

'Oh my God, there's a big scary tiger.' I say, pretending to hide behind Felix. The boy laughs and makes a roaring noise. Felix pretends to be scared too which makes the boy fall about laughing. I've never seen him with kids this young.

'It's face paint,' the boy explains. 'I'm not really a tiger.'

His mum smiles in thanks at us as they finish up and pay the painter.

'Do you want yours doing?' the face painter asks.

'Ah, thanks, I'd love to, but we don't have a penny left to our name.' I tell her. It's not entirely true, we have a quid left, but that's our last quid and so an emergency quid.

'Sophie.' The woman yells though the car window behind us. 'My friend is practising,' the woman says. 'If you're willing to be guinea pigs, she'll do it for free.' She looks at our faces. 'They'll look just as good, I'm sure. She's an artist. She just needs to be able to practice using the paints before we let her loose on the paying public.'

'Then yes please.' It must be my lucky day. I take a seat.

Sophie comes out of the car and the face painter whose name is Mandy explains we're volunteers. Sophie looks at us and grins. 'I'm going to do you as an angel and him as a devil. He has that wicked look about him.'

'Ha she's got you pegged.' I goad Felix, secretly wishing *every* female didn't flirt with him.

'Who, me? I'm never naughty,' he says, with a mischievous twinkle in his eye.

Sophie stares back at him hungrily. I feel a tightening in my throat and the words *'back off, bitch'* come into my mind. Whoa! I can't be getting jealous over a total manwhore like Felix. It must be the alcohol.

Sophie puts a pale white all over my face and then paints elaborate angel wings using silver and light blues over my eyes.

'Oh my God, thank you.' I tell her, not able to drag my eyes away from the mirror she holds up. It's absolutely beautiful. 'You are really talented. Both of you,' I add as I don't want Mandy feeling jealous.

She smiles. 'Come on then, devil, let's have you,' she says. There's a definite flirt to her tone. Little whore.

I hold my stomach. 'Felix. I think I just felt the baby kick.' His eyes widen to twice the size. Ha, ha, that'll stop her getting into his pants. 'Here,' I grab for his hand. 'Can you feel it?'

Felix eyes become bemused. 'Oh my God. Really, my angel?' he asks theatrically. He holds his hand on my stomach. It feels weird having his hands on me. 'Was that one then?' he asks excitedly. 'Was that a tiny flutter, or is it wind?'

'It's a flutter.' I tell him pointedly.

'You don't look pregnant,' Sophie says, eyeing me suspiciously.

'She doesn't, does she? It's because she's an athlete. Super fit and still runs every day.'

I'm going to kill him.

'Ah, okay.' Sophie's lost all enthusiasm for face painting now she knows she's not going to get some. She paints Felix's face bright red and then adds black wings at the edge of his eyes. A quick bit of black paint added to his eyebrows and a goatee beard. 'All done.'

Felix looks a tad disappointed but soon picks himself back up.

'Thank you so much.' He says, giving both ladies a peck on the cheek. 'Now, come on, Angel, you've not done as much running today. You must keep it up. We don't want you getting chubby.'

The women look back at him, horrified.

'Yes, you're so right, darling.' I say through gritted teeth. I take off at a leisurely jog.

Felix sprints past me, 'Loser.' He yells.

I try to keep up, until we're out of sight of the face painters. We're near the harbour now and I find a bench and collapse back against it.

'You've fucking killed me.' I yell. 'I need to lie here a minute and get my breath back.'

'Must be the pregnancy knackering you out,' he says with a knowing wink. 'Was someone feeling a bit jealous back there?'

I scoff. 'Don't be ridiculous!'

'Okay, if you say so. I'm going to wander around the amusements across the street. Don't worry, I'm not spending. Just had an idea.'

I'm too tired to argue.

It's a bit breezy, so I pull my feet up on the bench and place my arms around my knees. After ten minutes there's still no sign of Felix and I'm getting chilly now. I look around but the only thing I can see is an abandoned newspaper. Don't the homeless use newspaper to keep themselves warm? I go to get it and lie back on the bench, tucking my bag under my head like a pillow and then look around, making sure there's no one watching me as I tuck a bit of newspaper around the top half of my body.

When I'm done, I do actually feel a bit warmer. I think I'll just put a piece over my head for a minute to block that breeze out of my face. Surely, he can't be much longer? What the hell is he doing?

'Look, Monty, there's one of those less fortunate people I was telling you about. Now stay there and watch mummy. I always try to help people.'

Aww, I think from under my newspaper. I do that. If I see a homeless person I always buy a big issue, or if they're on the street, I buy them some food from the nearest shop. I want to show myself and smile but figure an angel popping out from under a newspaper would make the poor kid jump. Then a slow realisation takes over me. Fuck, do they think *I'm* the homeless person? I lie very, very, still. A voice sounds near my body.

'I don't know if you are awake or asleep, but I can see you're breathing so that's good. So, I'm leaving some money beside you on the bench. I'll just tuck it under the newspaper so no-one else steals it. I hope you buy food, but I do understand when things are desperate that alcohol gets you through the night. Hell, I know, I sometimes need one once I've got Monty in bed, so no judgement. I hope your situation improves.' Then I feel a press against my abdomen and hear footsteps moving away with an 'Oh mummy that was so kind.'

I decide to wait for another few minutes to make sure the coast is clear.

'What the fuck are you doing, Katy?' Felix's voice is at the side of my head. I pull off all the newspaper having first reached under it and put the twenty-pound note into my hand.

'I was cold, and it seemed a good idea. Where the fuck have you been?'

'I've been hanging around the amusements waiting for people to leave and looking in the trays to see if they left anything behind. Sometimes coins drop down afterwards.' He holds his hand open proudly, '£1.26.'

I stand up and stuff the newspaper back into the bin.

'Where have you got twenty pounds from?' Felix gawps at my hand.

'Turns out I made more money just laying here.'

He rolls his eyes. 'That's women all over.'

We agree that we'll save the £1.26 and fill the car up with the twenty quids worth of petrol. We also agree that once we have money again we'll both give a tenner to someone who is genuinely homeless to make us feel less guilty.

'Come on,' Felix says. 'You can use this twenty-six pence worth of two pences in the slots. I know how much you like Tipping Point.'

'We sure know how to live,' I say sarcastically.

I win a One Direction elastic bracelet and wear it with pride as we walk back to the hotel.

'It's been a great night, hasn't it?' I state to Felix.

'It really has. I've had a lot of fun,' he says in surprise. 'And look,' he points to the wardrobe. 'All our clothes are hung up ready for the interviews tomorrow and we're back at a reasonable time of night. Let's get ourselves ready for bed and get a good night's sleep.' He pauses. 'Do you think you'll manage to sleep seeing as you've already had a power nap?'

'Yeah,' I yawn, proving I'm still tired. 'It must be my delicate condition.'

Felix goes to the bathroom and stays in there for over ten minutes. I figure he must be wanking. What else could he be doing for that long?

He finally comes out, his face still painted. He must have forgotten with all the wanking.

'You've not done a very good job on that, Felix. Your face is still red.' I tell him with a straight face.

'You reckon?' He says sarcastically. 'The black bits came straight off, but the red base has hardly shifted.'

'Here, use my cleanser,' I tell him, throwing him the bottle, 'but leave some for me. You only need a fifty pence piece size.'

A few minutes later, he re-emerges from the bathroom. 'It's still not coming off,' he tells me on a heavy sigh.

I start laughing. 'Oh my God, you might have to attend the interview looking like you've stayed out in the sun too long today. You look burnt.'

'You've not tried taking yours off yet, *Angel*.' He says with a sneer.

I roll my eyes. He's obviously being ridiculous. I take my cleanser into the bathroom and remove the angel wings easily, but my white face remains. I look like the undead.

'This is fucking ridiculous. Why is it not coming off?' I yell.

He walks into the bathroom and stands behind me, so I can see him in the mirror.

'I don't know and I'm too bloody tired to think about it. We'll sort it in the morning. I'll Google it. Let's call it a night.' He stomps into bed and puts his head on the pillow. He's out in seconds. I decide to take his advice and crawl into bed myself.

## Chapter 13

Katy

It still won't come off. At least I have make up so after an hour of applying foundation over it I look... well, I still look deathly pale, but it's an improvement. I've tried to put some foundation on Felix's face but he looked like a demonic clown and so we cleansed it back off. It's a lot better than it was, but he still looks severely sunburnt.

We quickly have a coffee and a chocolate biscuit for breakfast and then we're on our way to our interviews at nine am and ten am.

As we pass the hotel receptionist, she calls out. 'Oh goodness. You really do look washed out this morning. I thought a comfy sleep might help. Have you had something to eat?'

I have to remember she thinks I'm pregnant.

I shake my head. 'No, I couldn't face anything.'

'Do you think you could handle a slice of toast?'

'Maybe.' I say thinking *yes fucking please*. 'God, now you've said that I'm in the mood for a bacon sandwich. God, cravings are the worst. We're going to be late now because I need to go get one right away.'

'Wait there.' She says, placing a finger across her lips.

Oh my God, it's working.

'You realise we're going to hell for all these lies, don't you?' Felix says with an amused quirk of his eyebrow.

I look at his red face. 'You're already there, mate. Must be karma.'

The receptionist comes skulking out with two wrapped sandwiches. 'Here, I know I stuffed my face when I had cravings. If not, I'm sure your husband would eat the other one.' She looks at Felix, her face contorting. 'My! You must be stressed. Your face is bright red.'

'God, you are like my guardian angel.' I tell her, taking the sandwiches and giving her a quick hug. When I back away she beams.

'Well, I'm guessing you have meetings or

something today. Don't work too hard. You need to rest to grow that baby.'

'Thank you again.' I say as we leave the building.

Once we're safely in the car, I hand over a bacon sandwich. 'Just be careful not to get greasy marks on your clothes.' I tell Felix who almost snatches the sandwich out of my hand. Moody pants.

The school looks really nice as we walk up the long, gravelled driveway. It apparently dates back to the eighteen hundreds and feels like it's been plucked straight out of Midsummer Murders. We've managed to keep our clothes clean which is a miracle with how things have been going against us lately.

The receptionist greets us with an apologetic smile on her face. 'I'm afraid Mrs Tibbins is running behind this morning as her car won't start.' Its then she notices our faces, her forehead frowning, clearly trying to work out what the hell happened to us.

'She's hoping to be here for ten am, so all the interviews are going to run thirty minutes behind. If you could take a seat in the waiting room,' she points to a door. 'The nine-thirty am interviewee is already in there.'

We knock and walk into the waiting room. Sitting there is a woman who looks to be in her mid-fifties. She has mid-brown wavy hair, between short and mid length; and really rosy chubby cheeks.

'Oooh, competition, just kidding!' She kind of singsongs. 'Sit down and we can have a singalong or something while we wait. Ha, only joking again.' She says with a laugh that contains a snort.

I may throat punch her, she's too fucking happy for words. Especially this early in the morning.

'Mavis Bromley.' She holds out a hand and Felix shakes it, so I follow suit. I can't be rude, can I?

'Oh my goodness,' she looks at Felix's face. 'Did your parents not tell you about applying sun lotion? I bet they did and I bet like mine you're all *"oh leave me alone, mother, I know what I'm doing"*, but do you? Do you? No, you go get a girl preg- I mean you get all sunburned. You'll have to keep an eye out on that now for skin cancer you know, and in future factor fifty, you just can't risk anything less.'

She looks at me. 'Like this lady here. You've used factor fifty or stayed completely in the shade haven't you, with that porcelain complexion? It'll keep you young looking, my dear.'

I take a seat, trying my hardest not to laugh.

'Right, well I think the least they can do if they're seeing us late is offer us a drink. I'll go place an order. What would you like?'

We tell her two coffees and she's out of the door in a flash.

'Fucking hell,' Felix says on an exhale as soon as she's out of the room. 'She never paused for breath.'

'This delay should be entertaining.' I tell him sarcastically.

When she comes back she tells us that she's going for the job as she believes it's her duty to help people in any way she can. That she left teaching for a while to help her husband set up a caravan business, but she realises that God blessed her with the ability to teach and when she saw this job she knew it was meant to be. Then she apologised to us for the fact she'd probably get it. *Unbelievable.*

Well two can play the crazy card.

'I had a message come to me in church, that I needed to apply,' I tell her. 'And then a little boy came up and handed me his toy boat and said it came from Scarborough and I thought, this is a sign.'

'Oh,' she says, her mouth closing for once. I should take a picture of her being speechless and post it to her husband. That's one for the fridge.

Felix rolls his eyes behind her, with a grin.

'So, what's this about you having a caravan business? That sounds exciting,' Felix asks.

What the fuck is he doing encouraging her to talk?

'Oh yes, we have them here in Scarborough where we live, then there's a few more in Skegness and some in Mablethorpe. Get to have holidays whenever we like. It's fabulous.'

'Though you'll not be able to do that if you get this job,' I point out.

'Oh, there are weekends and school holidays,' she says dismissively. 'Anyway, I have faith. Everything will turn out as it should.'

I wish I could be so bloody blindly optimistic.

'So where are you kids from?'

Felix launches into a complete crock of shit about us being made redundant from a school we were at. He says we have an interview in Skegness tomorrow but is *"not sure we'll make it as our finances have run right down and we may have to drive back home"*.' He puts on his puppy dog eyes. I have to admit they're effective.

'Oh, you poor things.' I swear you can see the cogs whirring in her head. 'I have a spare caravan in Skegness. You two are more than welcome to use it for a couple of days.'

Well, now I feel bad for thinking so badly of her.

'It's clean but awaiting refurbishment, so it's a

little on the tatty side: broken cupboard doors and frayed material on the sofas. But I'm thinking that whoever gets the job today, I was sent here to meet the two of you and aid you on your journey. Now let me get you the address and key code for the key box.' She goes rifling through her large handbag.

Okay, so we're staying in a shit tip, but its free accommodation, right?

There's a knock on the door. 'Miss Cornish?' the receptionist calls. 'Would you like to come through for your interview?'

The interview—for the first time since I started this journey—goes really well. I leave with the impression they liked me, and I might just get the job. Thank bloody God.

I open the door to the waiting room and Mavis beams at me as the receptionist calls her name. 'May the best teacher win.' She says with a jolly shrug. 'Enjoy the caravan.'

I close the door behind her. 'Enjoy the caravan, huh?' I say to Felix. 'Ripped up shit. I can't wait.'

He narrows his eyes at me. 'Katy, I thought you were living by the seat of your pants?' he chides me.

'Yeah, with my arse on a comfy cushion.' I complain.

'Well, never fear, because your stunningly

handsome companion has done it again.' He looks very, very smug. I want to smack the smirk off his face. Or kiss it.

'Now what? Is there anyone you don't manage to charm?' I fold my arms across my waist and then realise what I just said. 'Except me of course, I'm immune.'

'If you say so,' he says annoyingly. 'Anyway, we now have an empty standard caravan and in turn I just have to spend a few hours on the old one. I'm quite handy and from the sounds of it it's straightening a few cupboards and stapling new fabric. She's told me the tools are hidden in the wardrobe in the van. So I now have two caravan codes and we're sleeping in the nice one. Or,' He says, with a mischievous twinkle to his eyes, 'I get the nice one and you're in the old one. Might make sense if you're immune to my charms. I don't want you to get infected.'

He wouldn't bloody dare.

'You're the one who looks infected.' I point to his face and laugh.

'Oh yeah,' Felix adds, 'that reminds me. Our last pound will be getting used. Apparently baby oil removes face paint. Mavis told me. So we need that and some cotton wool.'

'Well, I think we can safely say, I'm not getting that job,' Felix says as we walk out of the building.

'How come?'

'Because they kept staring at my bright red face. All of them. Like *really* staring. You could tell they were trying to work out if I was sunburned or had really bad blood pressure. One asked if I felt okay, because they could postpone the interview if I needed medical attention.'

I find myself laughing so hard I almost pee.

'So I'm guessing yours went okay?' he asks, clearly digging for information.

'Yes. I slapped myself around the cheeks a little just before I went through and it must have done the trick, along with my make-up. My interview went really well.' I tell him, trying not to openly brag. I don't want to sound too cocksure in case I don't get it.

I'm surprised when Felix puts an arm around me. 'Aww, I'm really pleased for you. I hope you get it.'

'Thank you.' I smile back at him, my eyes assessing whether he's about to shout, "*only joking, loser!*".

'So, what are we doing with the rest of the day

then?' Felix asks. 'It's only lunchtime, but once we buy the baby oil and cotton wool, we have no money and only a few bits left from what my mum gave me.'

'Let's just go play on the sand. It'll take our minds off our stomachs. Then we could go around all the amusements playing your "get the spare change" game.'

'Good idea.' He puts his arm through mine. 'Oh, what we've become. Let's go have some fun.'

I giggle and can't help but think what a little old married couple we've become. Forced to stay together, no sex and bickering constantly. Sounds like your average forty years married.

After cleaning our faces of the face paint, we head to the beach and find an abandoned bucket and spade which some brat must have abandoned mid-tantrum. Both are cracked but they'll do. We make a ton of sandcastles.

'Fancy burying me in the sand?'

I laugh. 'Do I fancy burying you? Oh, more than you know!'

He rolls his eyes. 'Stop pretending like you could survive without me.' He lies down, hands behind his head, as if he's about to fall asleep.

'Alright there, Prince? Aren't you worried I'll ruin your suit?' I tease.

'Nah, you can always clean it up with your pube sponge.'

I can't believe he just said that! My face heats up. I duck my head down to hide it and instead scoop up some sand and plonk it on his lap.

'I'm never going to live that down, am I?'

'Nope!' he laughs.

I'm tempted to force his glorious face under when he flicks sand in my eye.

'You bastard!'

He smiles cheekily back. 'Don't pretend you don't love it.'

And the worrying thing is I do. I'm in big trouble and I know it.

After that we paddle and build a moat around the sandcastles. For anyone looking on we could be mistaken for any other couple on holiday. Well, apart from the stiff suits.

After walking down the beach we come back up to the top of the road where we go in and out of all the amusements, managing to scrounge the grand sum of thirty pence.

We're just heading back to the hotel when my mobile phone rings. It's a withheld number. Could it be about a job?

'Hello?' I answer far too eagerly.

'Hello, this is Miss Herts from Scarborough school. I'm ringing up to say that competition for this post has been very strong and although Mrs Tibbins did like you, I'm afraid we've offered the position to someone else.'

My heart sinks. I felt sure I was in the running for that one.

'What's up?' asks Felix, but then his own phone rings so he answers, getting the answer to his own question.

'I'm sorry, Katy.' He says. 'I'm assuming you got the same call?'

I shrug. 'Sorry to you too. Anyway, no sense in brooding over it. Know any way of making thirty pence turn into profit?' I ask him, trying to lighten the mood. 'Maybe we could go try it in one of the slot machines, see if we can win anything?'

Felix holds up a finger. 'I've got an idea. Better prizes than the slots,' he says with a twinkle in his eye. 'Follow me.'

He heads back up to a shop we went into earlier that had a raffle on a table, raising money for an animal sanctuary. 'How much are tickets?' He asks.

'A strip of five is five pounds.' The woman says. 'Or one pound for one ticket.'

I see Felix's jaw drop in defeat. He turns to walk away.

'Hold on,' I say, rooting around in my bag. Sometimes I throw change in there. Let me see if there's anything in there. I lean on the main shop counter and scrabble around, finally finding three five pence pieces at the bottom of my bag. 'Sorry,' I admit to him. 'We're still short.'

'Okay, let's go,' he says, walking back out of the shop.

'I'm just going to hang around the amusements again, see if I can get any more money,' Felix says with a hopeful smile.

I sigh. 'We really are pathetic right now, you know? I shouldn't have used that twenty quid for petrol, then we wouldn't be in this mess.'

'Yeah but you can't keep putting stuff on your credit card.'

I look around, noticing a gang of six pissed up lads walking down the street. 'You go in the amusements then, I'll wait here.' I lie.

As soon as he's gone, I walk up to the lads. I unbutton my top button to show the girls off and swing my hips. As predictable as drunk boys are they catcall as I walk past.

'Hey boys.' I say. 'I'll flash you my tits for a fiver.'

'Fuck off.' One of them says and they start walking on.

But one who's staggering more than the rest of them lingers back, patting himself down trying to find his wallet. 'My missus hardly ever shows me her puppies anymore,' he says, 'plus they're a bit saggy.' He hands me a fiver. 'I wanna really good look.'

I snatch the fiver off him and unbutton another two buttons on my shirt, so he can look over and see down without me showing my tits off to the whole of Scarborough.

'God they're beautiful,' He says with a wondrous look in his eye. He looks just about to dive in to motorboat them when his friends shout him, and he rushes off ahead not giving me a second glance.

I immediately feel a huge amount of shame about what I just did. What the hell has my life come to?

But that's nothing as to the look on Felix's face when his hand grips my arm and I'm spun around to face him.

His mouth is in a snarl, anger emanating from every pore.

'I don't care if I have to beg to wash up in a café or on the street, but you will never, EVER, do that again. Do you hear me? They could have dragged you off and attacked you and you are so NOT that girl. Now let's go.'

Wow. I didn't expect him to even care really, let alone become a protective bear. I keep my head down and stay silent. Nothing I say right now will make any of it better.

He walks me back to the shop, where the top raffle prize is a hamper. He hands over a quid that he must have found in the slots. 'One ticket please.' I keep my mouth shut about my fiver. He's obviously still livid.

'Pick from there, love.' The woman points to a bucket. 'If it ends in a five or a zero you're a winner.'

He picks one and I see his face break into a smile. 'I've won something.' He announces, looking around at the prizes. 'I've won, erm, Jenga.'

'Ooh, you'll enjoy that. All the pieces are there, I donated that myself.' Says the woman behind the counter. 'Well done, winning with only one ticket.'

'Yeah, thanks.' Felix says unenthusiastically, picking up the game. I follow him out.

'Well, we can't exactly feast on Jenga, can we?' He huffs.

Bless him. He obviously did think he was going to win something food related. That blind optimism can sometimes let him down.

'No, but we can go back to the hotel and play it. It gives us something to do tonight.' I say, trying to find a silver lining.

His mood doesn't seem to change so I offer an apology.

'Look, I'm sorry about what I did. As soon as I'd done it I regretted it. I won't prostitute myself again, I promise. But it's done now so can we please go get some food because I could eat my own arm.'

Felix sighs. 'What do you fancy with your prostitution money?'

'Large chip butties are £2.50?' I suggest, practically salivating at the thought of it.

'Lead the way,' he replies, his eyes lit up in excitement.

---

God, the chip butty was to die for and we saw a sign for *free scraps*, little bits of batter, so I asked for some and we ate those too. I still can't believe Felix had never heard of scraps before. I have them all the time. They're the tastiest bit sometimes. You should have seen his face when I suggested it; like I was offering him a Bush Tucker trial from *I'm a Celebrity*. But as predicted he loved them.

'Okay, let's go back to the hotel. We've got a bottle of voddie that your mum gave us. Let's get pissed!'

Felix looks at me with a wicked grin. 'We can play drunk Jenga!'

## Chapter 14

Felix

I ask at the hotel reception if they have a marker pen I can borrow and they manage to find me a Sharpie which is perfect. I head back to the room and sit next to the coffee table where Katy has put the Jenga box.

'What's drunk Jenga?' She asks.

'Right, well we write forfeits on every piece of Jenga. We'll split them between us, but they can be whatever you want. If you knock the whole lot down, you have to drink your entire drink down.'

'Okay, pass me that Sharpie,' she says. 'I'll be doing mine while you put your dressing gown on. I've washed the glasses so we're good to go.'

I laugh. Dressing gown. What is she like? I get changed into joggers and a tee shirt, relishing how she's now confident enough to get changed in the same room as me. She has her back to me and it's done quick as a flash, but it's still something. Something to prove the ice queen is thawing around me.

Once I've written my forfeits we place all the bricks writing side down and I stack them up into a pile and then we start to play.

Katy draws out **have a drink.** 'Ooh that's an easy one.'

I draw out **Truth or Dare**. She sits back and thinks about it, her mouth moving to one side.

'Truth. Have you ever done that back-to-back thing we did with anyone else?'

My eyes nearly burst out of their sockets. When we masturbated? I can't believe she's even acknowledged it happened, let alone asked the question.

'No.' I tell her honestly, locking eyes with her to show my sincerity. 'Just you.'

'Okay.' Her cheeks pinken. She's the cutest. What the fuck? Why am I finding a bird cute? What has she done to me?

She picks out another, **Make a sex noise**.

'Oh my God, how embarrassing. I don't want to. Can I drink all my drink again instead?'

'Katy,' I warn sternly. I love how she blushes on her neck whenever I'm stern with her. Then I'm imagining ordering her to bend over. Quickly, I clear my throat, trying to get a hold of myself. 'I heard you making lots of sex noises just the other night. I'm sure you can fake one.'

She goes even redder; it travels up to her cheeks. 'Okay. Well, I'm going to close my eyes to do it.'

Oh Jesus. I'm gonna end up coming in my pants.

I watch as she clears her throat, closes her eyes and starts to make those cute little noises I heard just the other night. 'Oh, oh, oh, God, yes. Just there, ooh yeah.'

My dick instantly tries to punch a hole through my boxers, straining against my flimsy joggers. Dammit, why aren't I wearing jeans?

'There, I did it.' She says triumphantly, eyes wide open. 'Your turn.'

'I'm not making a sex noise.' I protest.

'No, stupid. Your turn to withdraw a piece,' she says with a chuckle.

Ah. That would make more sense. Stop thinking with your dick, Felix.

'Although I've heard yours too, and it's more of a grunt.'

'A grunt?' I repeat, amused.

'Yep, like unnnnnggggggghhhh!' She pulls the cutest face while doing the impression. There I go again finding her cute. What is happening to me? I pull out another piece.

**Sit on player to your rights lap for a round.**

Well shit. I obviously wrote this for her to sit on my lap. She'll die under my weight. I hold it out for her to read and she giggles.

'Come on then, big boy,' she jokes, patting her lap.

I move over and position myself over her, but squat so I'm not actually placing my full weight on her. I would no joke kill her.

'Hurry up, and draw yours or my legs will collapse and I'll crush you.'

My close proximity to her body is doing nothing to make my huge boner deflate. She hasn't mentioned it and I'm glad.

She tries to reach past me laughing. 'This is like a weird version of Twister.' In trying to get around me she knocks the whole lot over. 'Damn it.'

'Ha! You have to drink a whole drink. Let me fill you up.' I say, grabbing the vodka.

'Ooh-err,' she responds and then that blush returns to her cheeks. 'Sorry, I went a bit pervy Keith Lemon there for a minute. I'll be rubbing my thighs next.'

Okay now I'm getting a serious case of blue balls.

She drinks her drink down while I stack the Jenga back up.

'Okay, you go first because you lost.' I tell her.

She draws out a brick. **Compliment one member of the opposite sex.**

'Oh, God, you're going to get so bigheaded.' She sighs. 'Like it's possible to get any bigger.'

I give her my best cheeky wink. 'Come on. I can take it.'

'Okay. Well, as far as I've seen so far and that's not too many, you have the best knob I've seen in terms of length and width and well… pinkness.'

My mouth drops open. Of all the compliments I expected, THIS WAS NOT ONE OF THEM! She's complimenting my *dick?!*

'I mean, I know none of them are what you'd call pretty,' she explains with a giggle, 'but yours is the best of a bad bunch, okay?'

I clear my throat. 'Erm, yes, thank you very

much.' I drink down my entire glass full of vodka. I bloody need it.

Katy tilts her head to one side. 'You're not supposed to drink unless the game says so, *stoopid*.'

'Oh, yeah, silly me. I forgot.' This girl is going to be the death of me.

I take the next brick. **Lick someone's neck.** Oh, come on, fuck off. Why did I write this? I wasn't thinking straight. I show her the brick.

'Ewww.' She says, her face curling up. 'Do you have to?'

'Yes, the brick says so.' I point to it to show proof.

She pulls her hair away from her neck and tilts it up towards me. I feel like a vampire going in for the kill. The closer I get the more I can smell her. She smells of lavender and mint. My God, it's intoxicating.

I lick slowly up the side of her neck, forcing myself to stop just below her ear. The urge to grab her hair and pull it back exposing her to me more is strong, but you know, I'd probably get done for sexual assault.

'Oooh, it tickles.' She giggles. 'Okay, my turn.'

**Finish your drink.**

'Oh my God, I'm gonna be hammered!' She slugs it down and refills.

I take the next. **Bottoms up.** I drink and refill my drink.

Katy draws out **arm wrestle**. She rolls up her sleeve and puts her arm on the table. I do the same and knock her arm over in 3 seconds flat. She sits back against the chair giggling.

'I love drunk Jenga!' She declares. 'God, I'm having fun, Felix, fun!'

I can't help but laugh along with her. I love drunk Katy. I mean like. I *like* drunk Katy.

My next brick says **confession** so I turn to her and say. 'Okay, the truth is I've been hiding a major boner from you half the night.'

'How rude.' She declares and falls about laughing again. Something tells me vodka and not too much food is having an effect on her. 'You haven't done very well hiding it! But I suppose when it's that big it's hard to.'

'Don't forget its pinkness, too,' I tease, replaying her words back to her.

She cringes, hiding her face with her hands. 'My turn.' She looks at her withdrawn brick. 'Hahahaha, this is NOT going to help with your boner, mister.'

She reveals the words **lap dance for 10**

**seconds**. Oh God. I groan. My dick is going to fucking explode.

She removes her towelling robe, dropping it to the floor, leaving her in just a camisole top and her panties.

Fuck. Me.

She stands near me and does what she thinks is a sexy swing and pose near to me, tilting her crotch towards me and biting her teeth. To be honest I've seen sexier false teeth. She sits back down. Well, my dick won't explode with that lap dance.

I lean over to take the next brick.

'Bet you've come in your pants now. You're welcome.' She yells. I jump with a start and knock the goddamn bricks over. Fuck.

'Drink up. Drink it all up.' She says, pouring the vodka high in my glass. 'Your turn because you lost.' She announces building it back up. It takes her two attempts. This is getting messy. Maybe we should stop soon.

**Take top off for the entire game.**

'Whoo hoo. Get it off, get it off.' She chants.

I remove my tee so I'm sitting in just my boxers and can't help noticing that she's staring at the shape of my dick beneath. The bitch is gagging for my cock.

'Bottoms up,' she yells, necking her drink. 'Your turn.'

**Twerk for 30 seconds.** She's written this one. Jeez.

I turn around and do my best to shake my arse. Katy doesn't say a word. I thought she'd burst out laughing. When I turn back around she's just staring at me and licking her lips. Did that weird arse dance actually turn her on?

'Your turn.' I tell her.

She pulls a brick out slowly—**body shot**.

I watch as she clumsily knocks all the bricks off the coffee table and lays across it, lifting up her cami. Oh my God. She's smashed.

'Come on, Felix.' She says. 'Fuck this game now, I'm bored with it. I can think of much better games to play. Now pour that vodka in my belly button.'

I don't bother telling her that she was supposed to TAKE the body shot.

I pour a drop of vodka in her belly button and suck it out. Jesus, her skin is so silky soft.

She grabs hold of my head and lifts my mouth towards hers until I'm staring down at her.

That's it. I can't take any more.

I crush my mouth against hers, my tongue capturing her own, making her mine. The coffee table is so damn uncomfortable, so I pick her up and throw her on the bed.

'I'm going to taste you somewhere else.' I tell her.

She smiles back at me, devilish intent in her eyes.

Moving myself down her body I place myself between her thighs, ease down her panties and throw them on the floor. I hover above her warm heat. This woman is going to kill me.

Dipping my tongue towards her core, I lick slowly up her seam. She thrusts her hips up closer to my mouth.

'Oh my God,' she gasps.

I suck and bite on her clit causing her to make those noises again, the ones she impersonated earlier except now they are oh so real.

'Oh God, Oh God, please, yes, more, right there, more. Don't stop, don't stop.'

I fucking love the sound of her begging me. I dart my tongue inside her opening. She makes a small squeal and fists her hands in my hair, pulling me closer to her core. I'm guessing she's near as her pants are coming thick and fast.

I push my hand into my boxers and fist my cock while I go to town between her legs. She's so bloody responsive. I bet that dick never did this to her. It makes me mad to think she stayed with such a loser who didn't appreciate her for so long. She tenses and then bucks into my mouth, shattering over me, screaming my name, before lying limp against the bed.

'Oh my God,' she gasps.

I smile back at her triumphantly, travelling up her body and laying down beside her.

'Felix. Do you want me to do you?' she offers, her eyelids heavy. 'I'm dead, but I will.'

'I'm fine. Give me a minute.' I jerk off into my hand, only needing a few thrusts before I'm coming in my boxers.

I head to the bathroom to clean myself up and when I come back she's sound asleep, snoring softly. I stand for a moment looking at her, her pussy on display to me in all her naked glory. She's fucking gorgeous. How has it taken me so long to realise?

I pull the covers up over her and climb in the other side. There's no way I'd have done the deed with her tonight. I want her sober when that happens—if that happens.

The only thing I'm sure of right now is that I really WANT it to happen. But when she finds out my secrets that will ruin everything.

I decide to push it all to the back of my mind and get some sleep.

# Chapter 15

### Katy

Oh my God. That's the first thought that runs through my brain when I first awaken. When I notice my head is pounding and my mouth feels like I licked the carpet. Licked. Licked... What's with that word? Why is it ringing a bell?

OH. MY. GOD.

I half open one eye to look at Felix who is still fast asleep. His mouth. I let him put his mouth down... there. I'm so screwed. Because:

I. LOVED. IT.

However, I decide what I'm going to do is not mention it, unless he does. Because I'm a little embarrassed that I've had his face between my legs. I mean, it's such an intimate thing to do. I'd half have preferred to have shagged him. What am I going to do if he wakes up grinning at me? I turn to find HE'S WOKEN UP AND HE'S GRINNING AT ME.

'Morning, gorgeous.'

'Morning.' I gulp. Quickly, think of something to talk about. 'Well, the weather's looking good... so I think we should pack and be on our way to Skeggy because it's my favourite seaside place in the whole world,' I ramble nervously, 'and you've got work to do on the caravan so I'm just going to go in the shower now...'

He pulls me towards him, right snuggled up into his arms. Naked. Skin on skin.

'Ah, let's just lay here a minute, shall we? We're toasty warm in our lovely hotel room.'

Yes, toasty warm and I can feel your morning wood on my leg. This is beyond awkward. I can't believe I've put myself in this situation. He clearly now thinks I'm going to be constantly up for it.

'No, no. I need a shower and to brush my teeth. Then we need to check out and get on our way.' I untangle myself and jump out of bed, still clutching the duvet to cover my modesty. Only it drags it off him too, exposing his glorious dick. 'Chop, chop, things to do!'

Felix raises his head up on his hands looking bemused. 'Are you avoiding me, Kitty Kat?'

I fight the duvet cover that is somehow trapped under my feet. 'Damn duvet, it's got frikking tentacles or something. Get off me.' I finally fight my way out, still managing to cover myself.

'Katy,' Felix says sternly.

'What?' I reply exasperated. I just want to escape. Run back home to my parents' house. Except they don't even live there anymore.

'You can avoid me all you like, but I'm not going to forget that I tasted you last night.' He licks his lips, raising his eyebrows suggestively. 'And you were delicious.'

'Lalalalalala' I put my hands over my ears like I'm a toddler, the duvet dropping down in the process. 'Agh!' I run off into the bathroom slamming the door behind me.

---

## Felix

I throw my head back onto the bed and sigh.

Was it too much to hope that she might wake up and not panic? That dickhead has a lot to answer for. She doesn't trust me, and I can't blame her really. My own reputation doesn't help. Looks like I'm just going to have to take it slow with Miss Cornish. Oh well. I stretch back my arms behind my head. I've always loved foreplay.

We're both hungry and our cheerleading receptionist isn't on duty, so we don't get a bacon sandwich, but escape a grilling (couldn't resist that one). Having not used anything we need to pay extra for, it's just card keys in a box and out the door.

'Get the car started and ready,' I tell Katy. 'I'm going to try something. Do we have a carrier bag? I might be ten minutes.'

'God, you're always disappearing,' she says eyeing me suspiciously. 'I don't think they have slot machines here.'

'No, but they have a buffet restaurant,' I tell her. 'So, prepare in case I need to make my escape.'

Her jaw falls open as I stuff the carrier bag in my pocket. 'You are shameless.'

'Says the prossie that flashed her tits,' I joke back.

Her face falls. Oh shit, I've hurt her feelings. She's a sensitive little flower.

'Just hurry up,' she snaps.

And a moody bitch.

Head held high I wander past the woman booking people in. 'Excuse me, Sir,' she says, reaching out to stop me.

'Hello again,' I reply as confidently as I can. 'Just going back to the wife. I forgot my phone.'

'Oh, okay,' She says with a frown, obviously dazzled and taken in by my confident smile. She goes to the next person in the queue.

I'm in. Phew.

Next I need to find a table. I spot two twentysomething women at a table. They're all hair extensions and darkened eyebrows. Most definitely went on the lash last night. Easy pickings.

'My mate's late down for breakfast, mind if we sit here though?' I ask with a cheeky smile.

'No, not at all,' one says, flicking her hair back. The other starts preening her hair. They exchange a glance.

'Right, I'll just go get some breakfast,' I tell them.

I might as well feed up while I'm here. I collect a full English but add to my tray two cereal boxes, some fruit, and a selection of Danish pastries. Then I add bread rolls, butter, salami, ham and cheese. Then I sit back down.

'I hope he makes it down,' I say with a fake worried frown. 'We had a right night on the lash. If not, you'll have to help me hide this stuff in a bag, so I can sneak it out to him.'

I chat to them about drinking and clubs, making

a lot of it up as I go along until I've finished my breakfast and had a quick coffee.

'Well, it doesn't look like he's coming. Can you keep watch while I stick this stuff in my bag?' I ask them.

'Yeah, sure,' one of them says, adjusting her cleavage.

'Do you know, I think he'd like a bacon butty, but I don't want to raise any more suspicion.'

'Oh, I'll get you one.' The other girl says. Her friend looks daggers, she obviously wants me to herself. Then she realises she's got me on her own.

'So, do you fancy meeting up later?' She asks, pursing her over glossed lips at me.

'Sure.' I pass her my phone. 'Put your number in there. Where are you planning to be later?'

The girl returns with a butty which she wraps in a napkin and places in my bag. She's also got two blueberry muffins and adds those too. What a sweetheart.

'So what's your friend called?' She asks.

'Err... Jack. You'll meet him later.' I lie.

'Here, put your number in my phone,' says the other girl. Aren't they eager beavers?

I type in a series of random digits along with my fake name and then get up to leave.

'See you tonight then, girls. Thanks for the help.'

I hand the phone back and get out of there as swiftly as possible before the girls suss out Mr Noah Chance isn't real.

As soon as I'm out of the hotel, I run to the car and jump in the passenger seat.

'Go!' I shout at Katy.

She stumbles around putting the car into drive and then wheel spins away.

'What is happening? Did you rob them or something?'

I laugh. 'Nah, but drive down the street fast and then find somewhere to park because I've a bacon sarnie with your name on it.'

'Mmm, I can smell it.' She says, her belly rumbling loudly. 'I love you, Mr Montague!'

I smile wide, watching her horrified reaction as she realises what she's just said. She blushes scarlet, quickly looking back on the road.

She parks up a few minutes away. I pass her the sandwich and she looks in the bag. 'Oh my God, you clever, clever man.' She leans over and kisses my cheek.

See, slow and steady wins the day with our Kitty Kat.

We arrive at the caravan park two-and-a-half hours later. It's small with only about twenty caravans on the entire site. We get the key from the keycode holder situated just inside the gate and pull up outside the one we're staying in. The caravan has a balcony around it with a table and chairs. If the weather stays nice, it will be lovely.

We unpack, getting a drink of water from the sink. Poor Katy has only had a drink in the hotel room this morning.

'God, I needed that. Bacon always makes me thirsty,' she tells me.

I'm thirsty. For her.

'There's a drop of vodka left, if you fancy it?' I tell her with a cheeky wink.

'I think I'll give that a miss for now,' she says with a grin. 'Oh, I need the bathroom.' With that she makes her escape.

I knock on the bathroom door. 'Katy. I'm going to take a look at the other caravan and see what needs doing. You chill out here and relax.'

'Okay.' She shouts back.

The other caravan is in need of attention, but as I'd hoped it's nothing screwdrivers, sandpaper, and some hard work won't sort out. I figure I may as well start now and let Katy have a rest. She's done the large part of the driving and must be knackered.

I start straightening cupboards and sanding them down. About an hour and a half later Katy comes and finds me, bringing a large mug of tea. The girl read my mind.

'We're in luck. The people who left the caravan have left a full pint of milk, some bread and there are two tins of spaghetti in the cupboard. We can have spag on toast for tea.'

'We're feasting like kings,' I say with a laugh.

'Anything I can do here?' She asks looking around.

'Nah. Just keep bringing me cups of tea like a good little housewife,' I say with a straight face, petting her on the head.

She smacks my arm. 'Behave yourself.'

'Oh, why start now?' I laugh. 'Now go relax and I'll be back in a few hours. Thanks for the tea.'

By the time I get back the cupboards are all sorted and ready for varnishing and I've removed the old upholstery from the sofa. Tomorrow Katy could do the varnishing if she's willing while I sort the sofa.

I find her sat on the sofa watching Escape to the Country.

'So,' I say flopping down next to her. 'Would you mind fixing the spag on toast for tea while I jump in the shower? Then you can show me this seaside town you love so much.'

'Have you never been to Skeg-vegas?' She asks, eyes wide.

I snort a laugh, shaking my head. 'Nope.'

'Well, Mr Montague, you are in for a treat.'

We eat out on the veranda. It's so pleasant looking out over green fields and we're only about twenty minutes walk from the front. I offer to take the car, but Katy reminds me that we need to use as little petrol as possible and that it's a lovely warm night anyway.

She shows me Skeg-vegas as she calls it. I feel really bad that we can't do pitch and putt, or visit the model village. There's a massive amusements on the front and we manage to find a handful of coins to put back in the machines, but it's not what she wanted me to see.

'My favourite is the seal sanctuary,' she says with a shy smile. 'It's right down there though. No point in us walking all that way when it's probably closed now, and we can't go anyway.'

'When I have a job.' I say, realising that I DO have a job, subject to references and thankfully I haven't included the Headmaster of the last school, 'I will bring you back here and you can show me the place properly. I want the full Skeg-vegas experience.'

She laughs. 'Okay, you're on.'

We walk back to the caravan.

'It's only nine. What are we going to do now?' She asks.

'Saturday night television and if it's a half decent caravan, there'll be tons of board games in the cupboard.'

Her face flashes with panic.

'No drunk Jenga, I promise.' I say in reassurance. She's a nervy little kitty tonight.

We get back to the caravan and I think I need to make it clear to her that despite what happened there's no pressure for anything more. She's obviously scared I'm going to jump her the minute her guard is down.

'Look, Katy. Last night I know we crossed a line and you're a little uncomfortable about it. I'm not. I enjoyed it and well, to be honest, when all this is done I'd quite like to take you out on a date, if you're up for it.' She starts to speak but I hold up my hand.

'You don't have to say anything now. If you said no it would put pressure on the rest of our days. Our focus is the interviews, I know. I'm going to sleep in the twin room tonight and you take the double on the end, okay?'

She nods her head. 'Thank you.'

'Right. Can we play KerPlunk now? I used to bloody love that game when I was small.'

## Chapter 16

KATY

Felix has been amazing. He was so gentlemanly and polite about what happened. He kind of cemented what I was feeling. I don't want anything upsetting our travels and potential career opportunities. That said, it's been lovely to have a weekend without an interview. Last night it was nice to just sit, chill, and chat, while we watched TV and played games.

But God I was so lonely in my bed without him last night. In fact, I have absolutely no wish to stay in bed and have a lie in when I know he's out there. I'll make us both a cup of tea and some toast.

I get out of bed and dressed but realise as I pass Felix's bedroom door that he's already gone. Oh. He's left me a note.

**Gone to caravan early to try to get finished as soon as possible. If you are up in time and fancy helping me varnish, then bring your lovely self over with a nice cuppa (pretty please).**

We've been in the caravan for an hour working when there's a knock at the door. It opens and a middle-aged man walks in, his arm outstretched.

'Well, hello there. You must be Felix and Katy. I'm Bill, Mavis' husband. Sorry I didn't get chance to come and say hello yesterday. I spend most of my time up in Scarborough.'

'Hi.' I shake his hand. 'Lovely to meet you.'

Felix rubs his hands down himself and does the same.

'I'm much obliged to you for this, son.' Says Bill. 'We're trying to get them done with a quick turnaround, but we keep being let down by folks.'

'Well, we're much obliged for the use of the caravan for a couple of nights.' Felix tells him, as polite as pie.

'Yeah, Mavis was saying that you were down on your luck a little. She got the job, you know?'

Of course she bloody did.

'So she knew you two didn't. Listen,' he says,

looking at his feet. 'We were talking and we want you to have this as well, for helping.' He reaches into his pocket and holds out a twenty-pound note.

'No mate,' Felix says with a shake of his head. 'You've given us the caravan and that's enough.'

Bill looks around the caravan. 'I understand you being a man of pride and I respect that. So how about you earn it by giving the cupboards in the bedroom a coat of varnish too?'

Felix looks at him as if torn. 'Oh, go on then.'

'We've got twenty quid!' I dance around the caravan once Bill has left. 'We're rich! Totally and utterly rich.'

Felix laughs. 'What has our life come to when twenty quid is like winning the lottery?'

I snort a laugh. 'We're going to have the best rest of the day and evening ever.'

'Now,' he says, clapping his hands together, 'let's get this varnishing finished and then we can go enjoy ourselves. On a budget, of course.'

---

First, I show Felix the seal sanctuary. We can't go in because it would waste our money and food is more important, but we still manage to see the adult seals through the door and a couple of meerkats. There's a gift shop around the reception so Felix drags me in saying he'll treat me to a cheap souvenir.

I choose a cheap pen with a seal on it as it will at least be useful. As we've just finished paying, another staff member comes up to the gift shop and takes over. As soon as the original assistant has left, Felix says to the new one, 'Do we just go through this door?'

'Yes, love,' she says, her eyes glancing over the receipt in his hand.

Oh my God, what is he doing? I follow him through the doors. 'Oh my God, Felix, I feel so bad because this is a charity.'

'Well, when you're working send them a donation. But for now, show me around the place you like so much.'

I want to tell him off, berate him a little, but instead I squeal with excitement. I drag him round showing him the cute meercats, the guinea pigs, the seal hospital, but mainly the damn cute seals.

'They're just the best thing ever, aren't they?!' I tell him.

He nods, a smile on his face.

There's a café and we use £5 of our money to get

some lunch and a drink. The sun is beating down on us as we sit outside the café. It's just blissful.

'Oh this is the life.' I tell Felix. 'Sitting in the sunshine and relaxing.'

'But after this relaxing, can we go to the fair please?' He pouts. 'I want a bit of the hustle and bustle.'

'Okay and you can spend £1.50, like I did on my pen.' I tell him. 'That will leave us with £12, right?'

'Yup.'

'Well there's a tin of spaghetti left so we can make do with that for tea. We could stretch to a loaf?' I query. I can't believe I'm asking if we can buy bread. It sucks to be poor.

'Let's worry about that later. For now we're at the seaside, our stomachs are full and we're around the cutest animals ever. Get your fill and then it's off to the fair because I have £1.50 to spend and I'm *very* excited about it.'

Felix follows me round while I spend another hour wishing I could have a pet seal. Maybe when I get a job.

After that we walk up to the fun fair. It's busy with music playing loudly.

'So what do you want to do with your money?' I ask him.

'I don't know yet.' He shouts back in my ear. 'But I think we should do some more dares. Get you out of your comfort zone.'

I laugh. 'Like what?'

'Like, go up to that group over there.' He points to what looks like a large family with several adults and kids, 'and fly around them with your arms outstretched making aeroplane noises.'

'What?' I gasp. 'You're crazy.'

'You're chicken.' He taunts. 'I knew you wouldn't do it.'

I look back over at the family, 'and if I do this? What's my reward?'

He grins, danger dancing in his eyes. 'You can dare me.'

Hmm, I could give him a real humdinger.

I take off, already with my arms outstretched and making noises before I get to them. I bump into several people who tutt at me, but I don't care. I'm in the zone.

'Neeoooooooooooooowwwwwwww.' I sweep past. One of the little boys in the group laughs and copies me.

'Elliott, stop it, stand still,' says his mum, giving me a dirty look. I do a final sweep just to piss her off before 'flying' back to Felix.

He claps on my return, smiling at me fondly. 'How do you feel right now, Miss Cornish? After your flight?'

'Exhilarated.' I tell him, throwing my arms up into the sky. 'Maybe a little jet lagged. Right, your turn.' I whisper the dare in his ear.

'Oh my God. You can't be serious.' He says to me, his eyes widened in horror. 'Please don't make me do that.' I point at the food kiosk and walk over with him. We wait in the queue for a few minutes.

'Yes, love?' Says a woman in her mid-thirties and poor Felix, she happens to have a big rack. 'Hmmm, could you tell me how big your breasts are?' Felix deadpans, squirming only ever so slightly. I'm impressed at his front.

The woman looks at him horrified. 'I beg your pardon?'

'The chicken breasts.' He says, cool as a cucumber.

'Oh,' replies the woman, 'we only do drumsticks, love.'

'Oh,' he says back, 'Never mind. I'm a breast man.' Then we walk off.

Out of earshot we start giggling. I can't believe he did it so well!

'This is so much fun, and it's free.' I tell him, jumping up and down from the adrenaline.

We walk up the sea front enjoying the day. Felix stops outside one of those grabbing machines where you can play until you win a prize. Inside is a toy seal. It's £2.

'Can I use an extra 50p please?' He asks with puppy dog eyes.

'Okay then. Remaining budget £11.50.' I inform him.

It takes him four tries before my fluffy seal drops down.

He hands it to me. 'I'm sorry you can't have a real one, but here's a toy one. You can keep it and think of me.'

I can't help but beam back at him. He can be so cute sometimes.

'Not think of the sanctuary?' I ask jokingly, raising an eyebrow. 'Think of you?'

'Hey, I'm cute and cuddly as well,' he insists, bumping my shoulder.

God, I am in serious trouble of falling for this man.

'Now are you ready to go back to the van?' he asks. 'I've had an idea for tea.'

# ROAD TRIP

When we get back and open the door we're surprised to find a bottle of white wine on the table along with a 4-pack of beers. Against them is a note saying 'Thanks again. Bill & Mavis.'

And to think I judged that sweet hearted woman.

'Bloody hell, that's awesome.' Felix says. 'I could murder a beer.' He opens it and starts drinking in seconds.

I pour myself a glass of white wine and we sit out on our balcony watching the sun set.

'So, after the interviews in the morning, what are we going to do about somewhere to sleep in Newcastle? Do you think there'll be somewhere we can park up and sleep in the car?'

'I have an old Uni friend who lives in Newcastle, remember? I'll Facebook her tonight. See if she knows anywhere we can hang.'

'Her?' I ask, feeling my neck stiffen. It shouldn't bother me that it's a woman, but the newly obsessed Katy can't help but feel upset.

'Yeah, Eloise.' He smiles at the memory of her. 'She was such a riot.'

Such a riot. Code for slag he used to shag. I hate her already.

'Did you and her, you know?' I ask, as vaguely and unbothered as possible. I already know the answer. They definitely shagged.

Felix turns to me, his gaze lingering over me for a second or two longer than necessary.

'We had a snog a couple of times, but nothing more.' I raise my eyebrows, warning him not to lie to me. 'Well... maybe I groped her tit too.'

'Lovely!' I laugh.

'Right.' Felix gets up from his seat. 'Get the spaghetti cooked. I'll be back.'

He wanders off and I watch him moving away, my eyes firmly fixed on his butt as he walks. God, he's fit. Sighing, I go to cook the spaghetti.

I have two plates warming up on which to split the one pathetic tin of spaghetti when Felix comes back through the door with a large white paper bag.

'What's that?' I ask, worrying about our budget. 'We really shouldn't spend any more money.'

'I haven't.' He beams. 'I called at the chip shop on site and asked for scraps. We've got loads.'

I laugh. 'Look at you getting into the scraps.'

'Who knew they were so delicious?' he shrugs.

I pour out the spag and he adds half a plate of

scraps each. Then he tells me to carry the plates outside while he refills my glass and opens another can of beer.

'After you can have your blueberry muffin or an apple from earlier,' he says with a grin.

'We're living the high life, Felix.' I tell him, smiling playfully at him.

'We're eating utter crap and yet I'm the happiest I've been for a long time,' Felix says with a sincere smile. 'That's what I'm finding the strangest thing.'

'Yeah, I feel the same,' I agree. 'Stupid, isn't it?'

We sit in the heat on the veranda enjoying our spaghetti, scraps, and drinks. After clearing away the plates Felix brings out the other beers and the wine.

'You can have a beer you know, I've not claimed them all,' he says as I refill my wine.

'Nah, I'm enjoying this. Unless you want some wine?'

He shakes his head to say no.

I can't help but be intrigued as to why he's such a manwhore. I mean, I get that men have dicks they want to get wet, but why in our school? Where he works? It seems so unprofessional.

'So why have you slept with so many women at school?' I ask him, unable to stop myself. 'It was gonna have to be time for you to move on soon anyway, right? You can't dip your pen in the company ink.' I laugh at my own joke.

'I haven't,' he says defensively. 'And I wish gossips like you wouldn't spread that shit around.'

Wow. That hit a nerve.

He sighs, running his hand through his hair. 'But I did at the school before that and my reputation followed me.' He admits.

'So you *are* a manwhore.' I tease.

'Was. For a while.' He clarifies. There's a pause, while he takes a swig of beer and sweeps his tongue across his top lip. 'I had a bad break up. We'd been together for six years. Her and our families were pushing for us to get married and I know she wanted it too, but something kept stopping me from proposing. I ended it and it was nasty. She trashed my things and dragged my name through the mud. I didn't want to go through anything like that again and so I set out to just have some fun. And I did.'

Wowzas. He was in a six-year relationship? And from the sounds of it not a particularly healthy one. No wonder he didn't want anything to do with women after that. Well, apart from every hole being a goal.

I nod. 'I can understand that. Break ups are hard.'

I think back to Dick and everything I sacrificed

for him. The amount of times I waited for him to watch another Game of Thrones episode when I was gagging to find out what happened. He always put his needs before mine.

'So maybe that's what you need to do, you know, Katy?' he suggests with a cheeky wink, obviously trying to lighten the mood. 'That twat has been shagging your sister. Let loose yourself and enjoy life a little. Take all its pleasures by the balls.'

I take a sip of my wine, contemplating what he's saying. Does he mean for me to turn into some slut on the hunt for dick?

'Wherever you end up working, you're going to get a new group of men to flirt with, Kitty Kat.' He looks at me, his eyes finding mine. 'And I envy every single one of them already.'

Wow. His words speak straight to my vagina. Blame the wine, or the fact he mentioned my sister shagging Dick, but I need him right now.

I take hold of his hand and stand up. 'Come on.'

'Where are we going?' He asks, a frown marring his beautiful face.

I turn around and face him. 'Bedroom. You're right; telling me to live life and enjoy it. You are exactly right. But if I want to live life to the fullest right now, then I have to have you.'

His eyes nearly bulge out of their sockets.

'I don't care what happens in the future. But right now I'm sick of playing it safe. I want you inside me. It wasn't the same without your body near mine last night. I want you, Felix.'

He chucks me over his shoulder and runs towards the bedroom.

'You don't have to ask me twice,' he says with a slap of my bottom.

He plants my feet on the ground and we make hasty work of discarding our clothes. He pulls me towards him and fixes his mouth on mine, his plump lips warm and sensual. It feels right. Like he belongs there.

Lowering me to the bed he trails kisses all down my body, feeling between my thighs and finding my wet heat. After kissing and caressing each other for what seems like forever, Felix excuses himself to get a condom from his wallet. Back in the bedroom he sheathes himself and then climbing above me he pushes inside.

'Ohhh.'

I think I've died and gone to heaven. He feels fucking amazing, filling me up completely.

Felix thrusts deep while I grasp his fine ass, feeling his muscles as he moves. We barely break off kissing throughout. I can feel my breasts against that taut abdomen, while his fingers trail up the side of my body causing goosebumps. His finger moves to caress my clit while he's moving in and out of me and it's not long before I'm done for, my climax exploding and milking his cock so he himself erupts.

Gasping for breath, we hold each other tight, kissing for a moment until Felix collapses at my side. 'That was amazing,' he tells me. 'You have no idea how long I have wanted to do that.'

Pulling me into his arms, I rest there for a while recovering. Until we're ready for round two and round three and well, let's just say that Felix has to use another £4 of our budget on a pack of three condoms from a vending machine in the bar on the caravan site. We finally fall asleep after round four.

---

The next morning it's very tempting to not attend the interviews and just stay in bed and use the final two condoms, but we settle for a quickie and then hit the shower, packing up the car and hitting the road. We've one condom left, so I tell Felix that when we get to Newcastle I'll look up their sexual health services and go to collect some for free. I should be a girl scout, I'm that resourceful.

Once again, our interviews are back-to-back, so we take a seat in the waiting room and wait for Felix to be called in as he's first today. He's already kept feeling my arse on our way up the driveway and we had a job getting out of the car while snogging. Basically, we can't keep our hands off each other like the hormonal teenagers we normally teach. I should be ashamed of myself, but I'm not.

Felix called Eloise earlier, and she said she had one room with a single bed and the couch. I told Felix I seriously doubted we could share a single bed and reluctantly he agreed that he'd have to go on the couch. I volunteered, but he refused (thank God).

From there it's on to my parents' house where we've no chance of getting any sex while my mother faffs around Felix like he's the second coming. We're going to have to find somewhere. I'm sore but I already want him again.

'Did you just squeeze your thighs together, you dirty bitch?' says Felix, looking at my legs with a smirk. 'You're horny again, aren't you?'

'Ssh, someone might hear,' I say, embarrassed.

Felix moves his chair closer to mine. His hand creeps up the side of my skirt.

'Felix!'

'There's only us two here and look.' He throws his jacket across my lap a little. 'If anyone does come in, I'll just move my hand.'

I'm so turned on I could burst. What is it about this man that just makes me throw all sensible thoughts out of the window?

His finger slips past the leg of my panties and enters my wetness. He caresses it over my nub and I close my eyes and sigh. He dips, in and out, in and out. I begin thrusting my hips up to meet the demands of his fingers and I'm about to come when the door opens. Felix moves his fingers and slides the jacket away.

'Mr Montague?' A man I presume to be the Headteacher asks.

He rises up to go for his interview and the man in the doorway holds out his hand to shake. Felix stands there frozen. Oh shit. He has my juices on his fingers.

In a sudden mad moment, Felix steps forward and embraces the Headteacher instead, giving him a full-on hug. 'This is what we do where I come from,' he announces, looking like a mad man.

I stifle a giggle, moving on my seat to get comfortable, forgetting that a split second ago I was on the brink of an orgasm. My slutty body decides it's going for it as I shift my ass. The tremors begin to take me over and I shake and buck, the headteacher seeing it all.

'Miss Cornish. Do you have epilepsy or something? Was that some kind of fit? Just a moment Mr Montague, we need to get this lady to first aid.'

Despite my declarations of being fine, I'm taken to Matron and given a once over before being allowed to return to the waiting room; my excuse of having an itchy bottom and being embarrassed about it being accepted by the school nurse who said she was forever dealing with them.

Felix returns from the interview room.

'Are you *ohhhh*-kay?' He asks, winking. 'They'll be asking you to *come* through soon.' He chuckles. 'My interview was a bit of an anti-*climax*.'

I give him the middle finger as the door starts to open again.

'Later, babes. Concentrate on giving the interview your all. Finish in style.' He laughs as I turn and glare at him as I follow the headmaster.

Interviews over we get back in the car. I decide to drive the first leg of the journey.

Felix cannot stop laughing. It's very annoying and if he wasn't so handy with his fingers, I'd tell him to go fuck himself.

'It's not funny. If we'd have got caught can you imagine the scandal? We're on school property for God's sake. No more shenanigans now in public places. Oh my God, I nearly died.'

'You did. You had la petite mort—the little death.' Felix howls with laughing again.

I start the car otherwise I'm going to punch him in the nuts and I don't want to hurt what I might want to play with later.

After a while of just listening to the radio The Kooks come on. The lyric goes *'I fell in love at the seaside'*.

'Well?' Felix asks, leaning back in his chair with an adorable grin. 'Did you? Fall in love with me at the seaside?'

I laugh and ignore him. But I can't help wondering... did I?

## Chapter 17

KATY

We arrive outside Elouise's place at around three pm. Felix seems annoyingly excited to see her. It's pissing me off. What, was I not enough for him last night? Now he wants Elouise too? God, I hate that I like him enough to feel this jealous.

We ring the doorbell of the thin terrace house. Felix doesn't have his arms around me, but then I suppose he is carrying our suitcases. I wonder what she looks like?

The door swings open and a vision with a rush of red curls stands in front of us. You could sharpen your knives on her perfect cheekbones, her pale complexion like a porcelain doll's.

'Felix!' she exclaims, her arms jumping to around

his neck. A rush of flowery perfume hits me. 'How are you?' she asks, rocking him from side-to-side.

'Good, thanks, babe,' he says patting her back.

*Babe?* Ugh, he's the worst.

She pulls back and looks at me. 'And you must be his friend, Katy?' She throws me into a hug too. God, she's a hugger.

I lean back, waiting for Felix to correct her. To say I'm a little more than a friend now. But... nothing.

'So where should we put our stuff?' he asks, pushing the door open and going through.

Why is it the longer I'm here the more I'm questioning if us sleeping together has changed our relationship at all? Maybe he just thinks we're fuck buddies now? I mean, maybe the whole joke about falling in love at the seaside was just that, a joke? I could be reading far too much into everything. God, I hope I'm not coming across as clingy.

We leave our stuff in the sitting room while Elouise makes us a cup of tea, and some poached eggs on toast. I've changed my mind; I suppose she's okay. It helps that she is able to make the most perfect poached eggs. Something to do with adding salt she says.

'So do you guys fancy doing anything tonight?'

Felix grimaces at me. 'To be honest El, we're a bit skint. So we're happy just to chill here if that's okay?'

'Of course it is! I tell you what, I'll treat us to a Chinese.'

Oh my God, Chinese. I could kiss this woman.

'Are you sure?' I ask, feeling like a right ponce.

'Absolutely. Plus, that way I can embarrass Felix and show you lots of uni photos.'

My face lights up. 'Yes please!'

Then I remember I said I'd find a family planning clinic and get condoms. Not that I know when we'll next be using them.

'Oh, Felix, there was that other thing we said we'd do this afternoon... remember?' I raise my eyebrows, trying desperately to communicate telepathically with him.

He stares back at me blankly. God, he's a tool.

'You know... that... phone *protector* I wanted to buy.'

He frowns. 'Phone protector? You already have one. Why are you trying to spend money on crap like that when we're on a strict budget?'

He can be so dim sometimes. The fact he teaches children worries me no end.

'I'm just saying that I'd rather have the

*protection*, than not have it. Better to be *safe* than sorry, right?'

He finally seems to catch on. 'Oh, yes, right. I should go with her. You know, make sure she doesn't get ripped off.'

'Well I'll come too then!' Elouise beams. 'Show you my city.'

---

Of course she wanted to tag along. Luckily, according to Google maps, there's a clinic just off the high street. I just have to lose her for long enough. We're currently in a chocolate souvenir shop browsing. Talk about bring a girl to the river, but don't let her drink.

'How am I going to get away?' I whisper to Felix.

'I'm trying to think,' he whispers back, chewing his lip anxiously.

'Are you okay?' I blurt out, unable to take all of this uncertainty. 'I mean, you've been acting really distant since we got here.'

His face frowns. 'Sorry. I guess I'm just nervous of her gossiping back to my ex. They're still friends.'

'Oh, I see.'

Well thank God I asked. That's stopped me obsessing all night.

'I just don't want her to know my business.'

'Fair enough.'

'Here, why don't you sneak off now and I'll distract her?'

I raise my eyebrows. 'It's how you'll distract her that worries me.'

He grins. 'Promise. No touching of her vagina.'

I shiver. 'That's supposed to fill me with confidence?'

'Just go,' he grins, slapping me hard on the arse. So hard I yelp, causing half the shop to turn round and stare. Luckily Elouise is still stuck into conversation with the woman at the counter.

---

I arrive at the clinic out of breath. Hopefully I can just grab a couple of condoms from the front desk and get the hell out of there. I look around at the desk, but there's none out. Well this is a bloody disaster.

A woman comes out from the back.

'Hi,' I say as confidently as I can. 'I'm looking for some help.'

'Of course,' she nods understandably. 'Come with me.' She takes my arm and starts gently leading me into a room.

I sit down on a chair opposite her swivel one.

'Now, tell me, how are you feeling?' she asks, her eyes drooped in sympathy.

'Um... fine, thanks. And you?'

'Don't worry about me. We're here to support you.'

Ah. How lovely is she?

'Right, well...' I edge awkwardly on my chair. 'I'm just here for some condoms really.'

She frowns. 'Right. And tell me, do you often seek out sex when you're feeling low?'

'Err... no? I'm normally in a good mood when I want some.'

'Okay.' She makes some notes.

Jesus, why is she making notes? I just want some sodding condoms. Is this some kind of new policy?

'And do you have a sexual partner to use these condoms with? Someone you can trust? A boyfriend perhaps?'

'Um... well, we haven't had that discussion yet. It's all very new.'

She lowers her glasses. 'Can I just warn you that

it could be dangerous to your health to seek out comfort in the first man that comes along.'

I widen my eyes in horror. 'He's not the first man to come along!' Jesus, she's slut shaming me!

'Regardless, sometimes when we're feeling low we seek that physical comfort, but later regret the decision when the feeling seeps back. Especially when we choose sexual partners that don't fully understand us. Do you see what I'm getting at?'

'Er... kinda?'

'May I suggest a few things to try instead?'

I shrug. 'I'm all ears...'

'Weighted blankets are great. Sure they may be pricey, but they're great at making you feel supported. A bit like a person cuddling you.'

'Right... but I really do just want those condoms.'

'Are you on any medication?' she asks, consulting her screen.

'No. I just want the bloody condoms!'

'That's fine, Rachel. We just want to assess your mental health first.'

'Mental health?' I shriek. 'What on earth are you talking about? And why are you calling me Rachel?'

She looks at me with narrowed eyes. 'Because you called in and spoke to my assistant? About feeling suicidal and needing someone to talk to?'

'I'm really sorry, but my name is Katy and I just want some condoms. This is the sexual health clinic, right?'

Her face drops. 'Ah. I think I see the confusion now. This is only a sexual health clinic for three days a week. The rest of the time it's a mental health clinic.'

'Ah. So... about those condoms...'

---

We spend the evening in our pyjamas stuffing our faces with Chinese, laughing at old pictures and stories of Felix, and watching *Olympus Has Fallen*. I can't believe I judged Elouise so quickly. She's actually pretty bloody lovely.

'Right, I think I'm gonna go up to bed,' I say after a rather large yawn. It's been a while since I've had such a full tummy and its knackered me out.

I try to catch Felix's eyes to communicate that he's free to creep up later. He only seems to give me a quick nod and smile before looking back at the film. Well! He sure knows how to make a girl feel special. Funny how when you're not getting your dick wet your priorities change. Arsehole.

I go up to bed, but I can't settle. I keep tossing

and turning, wondering what the hell is up with Felix. Can he really just have dismissed me the minute Elouise turns up? I get that she's an old mate, and he'd want to catch up, but I haven't had any affection from him all afternoon and evening. It's making me feel needy.

That's it. I need to stop being such a girl and just go down and talk to him.

Creeping down the stairs, I'm careful to be quiet, knowing they open up straight into the living room where he'll be sleeping. I make it to the bottom step and spot the sofa when the floorboard creaks under my foot. I freeze, knowing it could wake him.

Only instead of his head popping up from behind it, it's Elouise's. What the...? Then Felix's head comes up after her, from under her, his eyes widening in horror when he spots me.

Holy. Fuck.

---

### Felix

I was just about to go up and see Katy when Elouise appeared in front of me in her nightwear. Only they weren't the pyjamas she was wearing earlier. This was some sexy satin nightdress shit, barely covering her tits, the spaghetti straps threatening to fall down any minute.

Before I knew what was happening she was climbing over me and kissing me. I was in so much shock, I completely froze up. Only then the creak in the floorboard made her stop and look up. I did too, far too late of course, because I caught Katy looking at me with hurt and betrayal present in her eyes. Fuck. From nightwear to nightmare.

She obviously thinks I'm some arsehole that sought this out. My reputation won't have helped things.

I think as quickly as I can, pushing Elouise off me, and running up the stairs after Katy, but my God, she's running like I'm on fire. Luckily, I used to run in school. I make it to her room just as she's slamming it shut. I wedge my hand in the door to stop her, but it doesn't stop her attempting to slam it shut.

SHIT.

My hand is crushed in the door, the noise almost as ear shattering as the pain throbbing through my entire body. A scream leaves my mouth completely of its own accord. I sound like a little girl.

The door opens slightly. I take my chance and

wrench my hand out of it, gasping as I look down at my crushed fingers. They're a dark shade of red, quickly turning purple. I look up to see Katy looking at me, her eyes wide with horror.

'Shit,' she says, reaching out to touch them.

'Agh!' I scream, pulling my hand away from her. I don't need her making it any worse.

I try to move my fingers in a pathetic attempt of helping the blood flow, but I can't move them at all. Every time I try to move them half an inch they throb in so much pain my eyes water.

'Come on,' she says, taking my other arm. 'We need to get some ice on them.'

I follow blindly. Thank God she's decided to forgive me for a few short minutes. I don't think I have the brain capacity right now to be in charge. The overwhelming urge to sit, rock, and cry in a corner, is creeping over me.

Katy leads me to the kitchen and starts running the cold tap. She pulls my hand under it, the sharp sting making me hiss. She walks over to the fridge and opens up the freezer, grabbing a pack of frozen peas, wrapping a tea towel around it and then pressing it to my hand.

'Ah, that feels good,' I admit, on a sigh, looking up into her concerned brown eyes.

They swoop away from me and down to the floor. 'It should start to feel better now.'

I nod. 'It already is. Thanks.'

Elouise walks in. 'Oh my God, Felix! What happened?'

Ugh, just what I need. Katy immediately swallows and looks uncomfortable.

'He shut his hand in the door,' she says quietly.

'Oh my God!' Elouise shrieks. 'Are you okay?'

Katy backs out of the room quickly.

'Katy, wait!' I call after her, but she's gone.

Elouise grimaces. 'Is something going on between you two?'

I look away. 'Huh?' I'm so not in the mood for this interrogation right now.

'It is, isn't it? That's why you weren't into the kiss?'

I sigh. 'Elouise, I'm sorry, but I'm not into you like that.'

'And you're into her?' she presses.

Ah, fuck it. I don't care if it gets back to my ex.

'Yeah,' I nod. 'I really am. But I'm pretty sure, with your help, I just fucked it up.'

She sighs, leaning on one hip. 'Then go fix it.'

I shake my head. 'If I've learnt anything about

Katy in this time together it's to know that she needs some time to cool down.'

'Just don't fuck this up, Felix. It's strange for you to look at anyone like that after Clare.'

Don't fuck it up. She's talking to the king of fucking everything up.

## Chapter 18

### KATY

I'm fuming. How dare Felix treat me like that? Like I'm some kind of disposable whore he can fuck and say sweet nothings to, only to then drop me when the next Geordie skank comes along. Well not this girl. I'm not here to be a vase he sticks his dick into when he's bored.

God, to think he actually had me thinking he might be interested in me. Actually like me for more than my tits and vagina. This road trip has clearly fucked with my head. I let my defences down and what did I get? Fucked over. Yet again. You'd think I'd learn from my mistakes.

At least I was expecting it with my sister. To a certain extent anyway. She never let me have anything for long before stealing it. I was stupid enough to think that Dick was mediocre enough to not be stolen. Hell, if things would have worked out with Felix, how long would have she left it before she stole him too?

I need to find a man I can trust. Someone I can rely on. Someone I can know won't go off to shag my sister when my back is turned. Goddamn it, I deserve someone that doesn't want to do that. Someone that only sees me in the room.

Yeah, I might not be a supermodel, I might have barely there boobs and a thick bottom, but I'm lovely damn it! There are far shittier people out there that get people to love them. God, I only need to turn on Jeremy Kyle to find awful looking people in relationships where guys love them so much they're asking for lie detectors because they think they'd cheat.

I was foolish to get involved with him for even a second.

After tossing and turning all night I decide I might as well get up. I chastise myself for hoping he'd come up to apologise last night. After he hurt his hand, he obviously decided he couldn't be bothered. I'm such an idiot falling for his charms.

So I decide to use this time to have a long leisurely shower, blow-dry my hair and prepare for my interview. Damn, that slag Elouise really is a good host. She even gave me a spare dressing gown and slippers.

I'm just going over possible interview questions when my stomach starts rumbling. Ugh, I'm going to have to eat. But that means going downstairs and having to face them both. They're probably in post-sexual bliss, it glowing from their pores. I'm not sure if I can take it. My stomach growls again. Oh well, there's no reasoning with it.

I stand up tall, pushing my shoulders back and walk down the stairs as confidently as I can. I can hear them talking in the kitchen, their murmurs finding their way out of the door. This is it. You can do this, Katy. You have nothing to be ashamed of.

I take a deep breath and open the door. Felix is sat at the kitchen table eating what looks like Coco Pops while Elouise butters toast at the counter. Felix is already fully dressed in his suit while Elouise is back in her fleecy pyjamas. Her hair is a glorious mess. That's what a night of sex will do to you.

I ignore them both, instead heading to where the box of Coco Pops is. I find a bowl and put some in with milk, sitting myself across the table from him. God, it's hard avoiding eye contact with him. I can practically feel his eyes on me, watching my every move.

'How did you sleep?' he asks.

God, just hearing his voice hurts. How is it just hearing it can make me want to cry all over again? I slowly push my eyes up to meet his devastatingly gorgeous face. It's really not fair for him to have that face. He should have a face as ugly as his cold, black heart.

'Fine, thank you,' I say, my voice cold and clipped.

He nods, his forehead frowned. 'Are you all packed? I assume we're still going to head straight to Edinburgh after the interview?'

God, he's a pig. He's only bothering to talk to me to check he's still okay to ride with me. In my car. And to stay at my parents' house. I should just ditch his sorry arse, but unlike him, I stick to my word.

'Yep. All packed.'

I look down at the cereal, no longer feeling hungry. Sighing, I force down another few mouthfuls before leaving to brush my teeth. I'm in the bathroom scrubbing at them when I hear his footsteps. I know it's him from the sound of his shoes.

I force myself to keep looking in the mirror as he walks behind me. He reaches around me, almost touching my waist to get to the toothpaste. His eyes find mine in the mirror, boring into me from behind. But I sweep my eyes down to the sink. I can't let him worm his way back in.

'Look, I'm sorry about last night,' he says, with a mouthful of toothpaste.

I'm forced to look up and into his penetrating eyes in the mirror.

'Sorry you got caught you mean,' I say through a mouthful of mine.

His eyes cast some sort of emotion in them before he quickly recovers himself.

'I didn't get caught doing anything. The only thing you saw was Elouise trying it on with me.'

I scoff, a bit of toothpaste foam falling out of my mouth. I quickly wipe it away with the back of my hand.

'You didn't look too distressed to have her straddling you on the sofa.'

'I woke up like that. I was just about to tell her—'

'Were you planning on doing that before or after you had your tongue down her throat?'

He sighs, grabs my shoulders and spins me around to face him, toothbrush still shoved in his mouth.

'I never once shoved my tongue down her throat.'

I shove him off to turn and spit in the sink. 'You didn't look like you were complaining at the time.'

He throws his toothbrush out of his mouth and spits in the sink.

'Look, I couldn't throw her off me and call her a crazy bitch when she's putting us up. I was going to do it a bit more gently than that.'

I sigh. 'Its fine Felix. I have absolutely no right to be angry with you. This,' I motion between us, 'isn't a thing. It's just two people passing time.'

His face falls. Yeah, he's clearly not used to being served.

'And thankfully for me, it's coming to a close. Just two more interviews and then we never have to see each other again.'

He bites his lip. 'If that's what you want.'

'That's what I want,' I confirm with a nod of my head.

---

# Felix

I can't believe she said that to me. That we were just passing time. I call bullshit. I know she was all in before. She's not the type to just shag around and I know she felt something for me. But I've obviously fucked it all up with the Elouise thing.

Shit, coming here was a massive mistake. But it's not like I knew she was going to attempt to jump me, is it? After seeing how furious she clearly still is its obvious I shouldn't have left her to cool down. I should have gone up to her room and demanded she hear me out.

The drive to the interview was horrific. Complete silence. The same while we waited. I only half arsed my interview. The truth is that I could head home to my parents in Harrow and wait out the summer for my new job to start. There's no need for me to be here at all. I'm just here for Katy. Damn, I must really like this girl.

Katy finally finishes her interview and comes out with a big grin on her face.

'Aced it?' I ask with a smile. Seeing her happy makes me happy.

She shrugs adorably, unable to hide her smile. 'I might feel a bit confident about this one,' she admits as we walk towards the car.

'Next stop your parents' house.'

'Yeah, listen...' She stops and turns to me.

Shit, is she going to tell me I can't stay?

'My parents won't leave me alone if we walk in

with this weird atmosphere between us, so can we, at least for tonight, act like normal?'

I smile. 'Is that normal, before we went on the road trip and used to kind of hate each other normal? Or normal, we have great sex and get on great normal?'

She blushes. Actually blushes. She's too cute.

'I just don't want them to see this weird atmosphere we've had since the Elouise incident.'

'Look Katy, I really am sorry. I honest to God didn't want Elouise to hit on me. I thought...' I kick the floor, 'I thought we had something good here? Don't we?'

She sighs, as if the weight of the world is on her shoulders. 'Maybe we did, but... it wasn't real, Felix. I can't trust you and I could never trust you. Last night just reinforced everything in my mind.'

'So you're going to let my reputation ruin what we could possibly have?'

'No. I'm just not letting another Dick mess me around. Pun intended.'

I could try to argue with her more, but I can see it in her eyes; she's shut down. There's no convincing her now. It's too soon after her being cheated on for her to try to trust someone. Let alone me.

## Katy

I'm looking forward to seeing my mum in her new house. They've moved to the cutest little two-bedroom mews house with green shutters on the windows. As I knock on the door the urge to see them settles on my heart heavier. I just want a hug from my mum.

The door swings open, my dad there with a big smile on his face.

'Hello, love. Hi, Felix.'

I throw myself into his arms, his familiar scent of Werther's Original soothing me like a warm blanket. I've missed him. It feels like far longer than eight days since I've seen him.

'How was the interview?' he asks, pulling back to look down at me with a concerned smile.

'It went great, thanks Dad.' I look behind him into the yellow painted sitting room. 'Is Mum here?'

'Yep. She's just upstairs.'

I smile quickly before finding the stairs and taking them two at a time, leaving Felix to make awkward conversation with Dad.

I find her sat at her dressing table blow-drying

her hair. Throwing my bag down I run to her. She must spot me in the mirror because she turns and stands up just in time for me to fall into her arms.

'Honey, what's wrong?' she asks, smoothing my hair down.

Tears start falling down my cheeks. 'Oh, Mum, it's just all such a mess.'

'What is?' she asks, leading me to sit down on the end of her bed. 'Are you worried that your interviews didn't go well?'

I scoff. 'The interviews are the least of my problems right now.'

'So, what is it?'

I take a deep breath, wondering if I'm prepared to tell her the truth.

'It's Felix.'

'Oh?' Her eyes have lit up in that way they get when she's excited. Damn it; I knew I shouldn't have told her.

'Before you start getting excitable, we're not together. And we never will be. I just...' I let out a heavy sigh. 'I just thought for maybe like a minute that I could be with him. That I could be happy again. Finally happy. But...'

'But what?'

'But he's just like every other guy out there,

Mum. Just interested in what he can get while he can get it. He doesn't want a relationship with me.'

'And why bloody wouldn't he?' she says, as if annoyed on my behalf.

'I don't know,' I shrug, wiping my nose with my sleeve. 'Because I'm boring. Safe. Predictable. Because my boobs are too small, and my butt is too chubby.'

'Your butt is not chubby!' she shouts, as if I insulted her own. 'And your boobs are a perfect size for your body shape. He'd be bloody lucky to have you.'

I laugh through the tears. 'You know, Mum, there comes a time where you just have to tell it to your daughter straight. Not give me all of this, "you're beautiful" crap. Actually, tell me why I continue to get shit on.'

She smiles. 'Katy, you are a silly billy. When are you going to realise that you're my daughter and it's impossible for me to see you badly? You'll always be the most beautiful young lady in the room to me.'

'Until Victoria comes in,' I snort.

She frowns. 'Katy, you know I don't love either of you more than the other. Even if your sister is harder to handle sometimes. But the only thing that holds you back, is comparing yourself to Victoria. You've always been in her shadow and it's like you've come to expect bad things to happen to you. With that attitude it will.'

I roll my eyes. 'It's learnt behaviour.'

'All I'm saying is that you shouldn't give up on something before it's even begun, because you're so sure it's not going to work.'

'You don't understand, Mum. He's a player. I could never trust him.'

She smiles kindly, like I have no idea about life. 'Tell me this. When he looks at you, do you feel like the only woman who has his attention?'

I think about it. 'Okay, yes, I do. But... I just don't know if I have it in me to put myself out there to be hurt again. What would you do?'

She smiles. 'Honey, if it was Felix, I'd be taking the risk. Have you seen that man?'

I burst out laughing. 'Mum! You are such a hussy!'

She throws her head back laughing. 'Did I ever tell you that your father was a bit of a lady's man?'

'No. No way? Dad?' I think of the Werther's Original smelling man I just left downstairs.

'Yep, your dad,' she nods. 'I managed to tie him down when everyone warned me away from him. In the end I knew that he was worth the risk.'

I can't believe Dad used to be a player. How embarrassing.

'Even if that risk means potentially breaking your heart into smithereens?'

'Honey, the heart can be battered and bruised, and at times it may feel broken, but it always withstands the pain. It keeps on beating regardless. It's the strongest organ we have for a reason. It knows sometimes we have to experience pain in order to find our true love.'

I throw myself back onto the bed, my hands covering my face. I just want to hide away from reality, but I don't even know if I have a bedroom here.

'You're going to have to face this, Katy. Whether you like it or not.'

I sit up and nod. 'I know. It's just that I don't know if he feels the same way and I can't bear the rejection.' The thought of him attempting to let me down gently has me feeling sick to the stomach.

She raises an eyebrow. 'Would you rather waste your life wondering what if? Trust me, life is long when you're wondering what could have been.'

I know she's right. But I'm not feeling brave enough right now.

'Okay. I'll speak to him, but later.'

'Fine. How about I run you a nice bubble bath in the meantime, cook us a curry and you can tell us all about your interviews.'

God, I could cry with relief.

'I love you, Mum.' I fling myself at her again, hugging her tight.

'Now, now,' she laughs. 'We might have moved, but we'll always be here for you girls, whenever you need us. You'll always have a home here.'

'Thank you.'

---

## Felix

Well I didn't expect Katy to bolt upstairs the minute we arrived. It left me, quite awkwardly, with her dad talking about the weather. Her Mum eventually came down to tell us she was feeling a little stressed and having a relaxing bath. The thought of her naked under those bubbles has my dick twitching. Must not get a hard-on in front of her parents.

'So, Felix,' her mum says with a smile. 'How did the interviews go?'

I give her a vague answer, grateful when she offers me some tea and biscuits.

'I hope you don't mind, but you'll have to share a room with Katy tonight. We've only got a two-bed now.'

'He can take the sofa,' her dad interrupts, clearly spooked at the idea of us sharing a bed.

'That sofa?' Her mum scoffs. 'Don't be ridiculous, Gerald. It's got more lumps on it than the Loch Ness monster.'

Nice Scottish reference.

I shrug, trying to come across as not too keen to sleep in her bed. Not that I even know she'll let me. She might tell me to piss off.

'I don't mind the sofa, if you prefer it?' I offer to her dad.

He looks at me suspiciously for a solid three seconds before nodding his head.

'The room share is fine. Obviously as long as no funny business takes place.'

'There'll be none of that,' I promise with an awkward nod.

I turn around to see Katy in a pink fluffy dressing gown, her hair in a towel. I smile shyly at her. I hate not knowing where we stand.

'Why don't you both take your stuff up to the room to unpack?' her mum says. Did I just imagine she gave me a wink? What was that about?

I nod and grab the bags, following Katy up the narrow stairs and down the hall into a small peach room with what looks like a barely double bed, and a dressing table.

I dump the bags on the floor and sit on the bed. She takes a seat on the stool in front of the dressing table.

'So...' she starts, wringing her hands together awkwardly.

'So?' I encourage.

God, just getting her to talk to me is painful.

She swallows, and I notice her lip is trembling.

'So I've been thinking...' she starts, unable to look me in the eye.

'Uh-oh,' I joke, just like I normally would.

She smiles, no doubt glad I've broken some of the tension.

'I was thinking about what you said to me. You know, about... us.'

My stomach clenches. What is she about to say? That we can't be together?

'Right... and... what have you decided?'

She folds her arms across her chest. 'Well, before I tell you, I want to know how you feel. What you want.'

Oh God. She wants me to lay it all out on the

table. Well, what if I do and she shits all over it? Tells me I'm a dick, and she doesn't want me anyway. I look at her face, her eyes squinted in vulnerability.

Here goes nothing.

'I like you, Katy,' I say simply.

'You like me?' she repeats, a grin creeping on her face. 'Like, as in you also like cheese? Or a different kind of like?'

'Okay,' I grin back. 'If you want me to be plain. I really like you. Want to take all your clothes off like you. Want to spoon you in bed every night like you. Make you laugh every day like you. That kind of like you.'

Her cheeks are practically puce they're so red. How can such a beautiful creature be so unsure of herself? That sister has a lot to answer for.

'Do you like me?' I can't help but ask.

She grins, her cheeks pinking up. 'I think it's pretty clear I like you.'

I can feel the shit-eating grin taking over my face. 'Like me like you like cheese?' I can't help but joke.

'More than cheese,' she smiles. 'But I'm scared.'

I frown. 'Of what?'

'Of you hurting me. I don't think I could take it if I was cheated on again.'

God, that dickhead really did a number on her

self-confidence. I stand up and walk over to her, dropping to my knees in front of her.

'Katy, I've never cheated on anyone and I don't intend to. I can't promise we'll be together the next twenty years, but I can promise that I'll spend every day trying to make you happy. Isn't that enough?'

She smiles. 'Okay. It's enough.'

## Chapter 19

### Katy

I'm so happy. I can't believe it took something as simple as laying it all out there to find out where I stand. Felix and I are together now; that's all that matters. He ended up parting my knees and going down on me right there on the dressing table stool. I think it was his way of apologising. I just really hope my dad didn't hear.

After orgasming against his hand to muffle the screams, he then decided to blow-dry my hair. It was strangely more intimate than any sex we've had. He was so gentle that I almost fell asleep.

We spent the night laughing and joking with Mum and Dad over a curry and then we stuck on Dirty Dancing. Waking up in his arms this morning knowing I'm his was heaven, but I can't help but have that niggling fear in the back of my mind. The thing is that we still have no idea about which jobs we're going to get. Where we'll be in a few months.

But I have to just ignore it and grab life by the balls. Enjoy the present and try my hardest not to worry about the future. Felix is in the shower while I relish still being in bed. It's funny how this immediately feels like home to me. It must be because my mum has such a good decorating touch. She makes everything so homey. The thought of living by myself frankly terrifies me.

Felix's phone starts ringing. I look at the screen. It's a withheld number. I could just let it go to his answerphone, but what if it's a job offer, and his phone doesn't record the message properly? I'd never be able to forgive myself. Fuck it. I press answer.

'Hello?'

'Hi, can I please speak to Mr Montague?' a woman asks.

'Sorry, he's unavailable at the moment, but can I take a message?'

'Oh, yes please. If you could just ask him to call back Harrow school. We haven't received his signed contract yet and we want a firm start date before we break up for the summer.'

Wait, I'm confused.

'Contract? As in, he has a job with you?'

'Yes.'

'Right... and he knows this?' I can't seem to get my head round this.

'Yes. Perhaps I've said too much. If you could please tell him to return my call at his earliest convenience.'

I hang up just as Felix walks out of the shower, a small towel tied round his waist. I can do nothing but stare dumbly back at him.

'Who was on the phone?' he asks, towel-drying his hair, not a care in the world.

I steel my jaw, a new anger broadsiding me. 'Harrow school.'

His face pales, his shoulders tensing. 'Oh.'

'Oh indeed. They asked if you could call them back.'

He relaxes slightly, obviously thinking that's it. Like I'm letting him off that easily.

'And that you haven't returned the contract yet. You know, for the job offer you've apparently had.'

'Er...'

'Er... what?' I shout, erupting like a volcano. 'How the fuck could you have not told me you got a job? And how the hell did you get one at Harrow? We acted like nutters.'

He sits down on the bed, his head in his hands. 'I went back in there and did another interview. They offered it to me on the spot.'

My mouth hangs open. 'You sneaky fucking bastard! Jeopardising my career and only thinking about yourself. How the hell am I supposed to trust you with anything, when you've done this?'

'That's why I was waiting to tell you,' he says taking my hand.

I throw it off me. 'What, wait until you'd buttered me up, and I'd just go, oh okay. Whatever you say, Felix. I'm not some little Stepford wife who's going to follow you around and wash your dirty socks.'

'Whoa!' he puts his hands up in self-defence. 'I never said that.'

'But it's what you meant. All that bullshit last night about us going wherever we get the jobs, it was all shit. You knew you had nothing to worry about. You're going home to your parents, to a town you were raised in. And you expected me to just follow on.'

'No. The reason I haven't sent back the contract yet is because I wanted to speak to you about it.'

'Yeah, right,' I snort. 'I don't know why I thought you'd changed. You're still the selfish manwhore you've always been. I wanted to see more, have some hope you were different, but leopards don't change their spots.'

'Ouch.'

'Get out.'

'What?' he blusters in disbelief.

'I said get out! I don't want you here. Go back to your mother in Harrow.'

'Katy, I'm in the middle of bloody Edinburgh. Where the hell do you expect me to go?'

'Ugh, you're so infuriating. You know what, I'm glad I told the Headmaster those pranks were all your fault. I can't believe I've been feeling bad about the whole thing.'

'You did what?' he shouts, his eyes nearly popping out of his skull. 'You blamed me? Katy, you're the one that approached me. I was just trying to help you.'

'Help me?' I scoff.

'Yeah, help you get out of your sad little bubble where you're stuck up your own arse. I even helped expose that fucking cheating creep. But it seems you're back to where we started.'

I repeat his words in my head. *Expose that fucking cheating creep.*

'Expose? What do you mean, expose?'

His face tightens, obviously realising his mistake.

'Did you... did you know Dick was cheating on me?'

He swallows. 'It looks bad, I know. But yeah. I overheard him in the pub and then I made sure that you'd catch him.'

'I cannot believe you! Why the hell couldn't you have just broken it to me gently, rather than to be forced to walk into the shit show that I did?'

'I'm sorry. If I'm honest, I hated you back then. You kept slagging me off around work.'

I gasp in disbelief. 'So you actually did that to me as revenge?'

He looks down at the floor, ashamed. 'Yes,' he admits on a whisper.

'How fucking dare you! Get out of my house!' I scream.

'This is your parents' house, and I'm pretty sure your mother wouldn't be as unreasonable as to chuck me out.'

'Ugh!' I scream. 'Just get out of my sight now, Felix. I can't believe I ever thought me and you could have something. We are so different.'

He grabs his bag. 'You're right there.' He slams the door in my face as I face dive the bed, punching the mattress like it's him.

## Chapter 20

### Katy

I stay in my room for the rest of the day, too upset to risk seeing him. I can't believe he did that to me. Totally screwed me over. There I was thinking we were in this together and the whole time he was just planning on moving back home and abandoning me.

I suppose it's my own fault for pinning my hopes on a manwhore like him. Who was I kidding? Of course he was going to shower me with attention and try it on when I was the only female he was travelling with. I was stupid to think I was special in any way. That's what guys like him do; they make you feel special, fuck you, then fuck off, never to be seen again.

I shouldn't have let myself get involved with anyone after Dick. Especially Felix Montague.

There's a light knock on the door. I sit up straight and dry my eyes. I don't want him to think I'm affected by him, to give him the satisfaction. He'd probably enjoy it, the sadistic bastard.

'Come in,' I shout lightly.

The door opens, but instead of Felix, it's my mum. She's carrying a plate of scrambled eggs on toast with a cup of tea. Damn, I love this woman. I can't believe they've moved away. And now I'm crying again.

'Oh, love.' She settles the tray on the side and sits next to me on the bed, wrapping me in a hug.

I have a good sob into her top. Oops, I hope it's not new. I get quite snotty when I'm crying.

She finally pulls back, probably soaked through to her bra.

'What on earths happened with you and Felix?'

'Oh Mum. It's all such a mess. I really don't know why I fell for him in the first place.'

She huffs a laugh, passing the tray of food to me. 'You fell for him because he's a charismatic young man. You'd have to be blind and stupid not to see that.'

I grab the fork and stuff a bit of egg in my mouth. Damn, no-one makes eggs like my mum.

'So what exactly happened?' Mum asks, trying not to act as eager as she is.

'Felix got the job in Harrow. He went back in and interviewed for it behind my back after he'd ruined my interview. He's nothing but a selfish, no-good bastard.'

I grab some toast and shove it in my mouth.

Mum strokes my hair. 'Don't be too hard on him, love. The man was desperate for a job. Just like you were.'

'Yeah, but I wouldn't have done that,' I protest before taking a sip of my tea. Ah, she always gives me an extra sugar when I'm sad. Then I remember I did try to leave him in bed the morning of that interview, so he didn't get there at all...

'Is it really worth throwing everything away just because he didn't tell you he had a job? Did he tell you why he kept it quiet?'

I think back to what he'd said about not having sent the contract back yet because he was going to discuss it with me. 'Am I being melodramatic? It just feels like such a betrayal.'

She rubs my shoulder. 'It's because you're so

loyal, you always have been. But I know that man is crazy about you and I personally think that if you don't swallow your pride and accept his apology you'll regret it for the rest of your life.'

I sigh. 'When did you get so wise?'

She laughs. 'You get a new bit of wisdom with every wrinkle you uncover. And look at my face. I've got a few!'

'Thanks, Mum. You're right. I'm gonna go get him now.'

I stand up. This must be love. Leaving my Mum's eggs to go to him.

'He's not here, love,' she says, as if she thought I already knew.

'Huh? Where the hell is he?'

'He said you'd told him to go. He apologised and then left. I had to loan him some money because he said you'd barely any money left.'

'What?' I jump up. 'Well, where did he go? Did he get a taxi? A train?'

She shrugs. 'I assume he got a train. It's a long way for a taxi.'

'Shit! How long ago?'

'Language, young lady,' she berates with a huff.

I grab the top of her arms, trying to communicate how important this is. 'Mum, when did he leave?'

'About half an hour ago.'

I grab my dressing gown and throw my slippers on. 'I can still catch him.'

She barks a laugh. 'There's no way you'll catch him.'

'Wanna bet?' I shout, already running down the stairs and grabbing my car keys.

I race through the door, throw myself into the car and put my foot to the metal. I run almost every red light, while trying to mentally remember how quickly trains to Edinburgh come. Every hour? Every half hour? God, the thought that I might have missed him has me feeling sick to my stomach.

I pull up outside, abandoning my car in a taxi bay and run inside. I've never been here before and I don't know why, but I expected with it being Scotland that it would be a lot smaller. But it's enormous. I force myself to concentrate on the huge board with the names of the destinations. I see London Kings Cross. Leaving in one minute. Shit.

I sprint towards platform seven, so fast I lose a slipper in the process and bound up the set of stairs. I see the train already in the platform. Crap. I push the automatic doors open, them going far too slowly for my liking, then I scan the busy platform, desperate to see his messy mop of hair.

I spot him down towards the end. At least I hope it's him. I run towards him, the crowd in front of him making their way onto the train. Luckily people seem to get out of my way. It's probably because I'm still in my pyjamas. I must look insane. But if I manage to get to him I stand a chance of making things right. I just know that if he gets on that train there'll be no going back for us.

I reach out towards him just as he's going to step onboard.

'Felix!' I scream, so loudly he jumps out of his skin. He goes to turn towards my girlish scream but must lose his footing. I watch as if in slow motion as his foot slips down into the gap between the train and the platform. Shit.

I watch in complete horror as one leg goes right through the gap, his torso flying onto the train.

'Agh!' he shouts, 'My balls! My fucking balls!'

People jump off the train and gather to help pull him up. We rest him, lying down onto the platform, him still clutching his crown jewels. His face contorts in pain, so red he could audition as a tomato.

I hover over him, but he's got his eyes shut in pain.

'Felix! Felix, are you okay?'

He peers one eye open. 'How the fuck do you think I am right now?'

I cringe. Yeah, hardly the best way to grab his attention. Try to amputate his dick.

'I'm so sorry. I just wanted to get your attention before you left.'

'Well you bloody managed that,' he croaks out.

A man in a train uniform is stood next to him. 'Do you think you need an ambulance, lad?'

He huffs out a big breath. 'Nah, I'm okay. I just...' he rolls over to his side and attempts to sit up. 'I just need a minute.'

'Aye, I'll hold the train.'

Shit. He's still planning on getting on the train?

'Why are you in your pyjamas?' he asks, as if he's just noticed.

'I came to stop you. Come back with me.'

'But I thought you wanted me to leave?' He looks towards the heavens. 'Fucking women and their mixed signals.'

'Aye,' the rail man nods, looking at me with distaste.

'Look, I'm sorry. But you have to admit, you did a shitty thing.'

He sighs. 'I know, I'm sorry. Truthfully, I was

going to tell you, but the more I liked you the more I was afraid of how you'd react. I mean, look at how you *did* react. The truth is that I was shitting myself about not getting a job and at the time I didn't think we were serious.'

'And you do now?' I ask shyly.

He sighs. 'I don't know. I mean, will you ever be able to trust me? You're always going to have this preconceived idea of me being some manwhore. We can't start a relationship with no trust.'

'I'm sorry. I do trust you. And I'm sorry I tried to get you to take the bullet in our school.'

He laughs. 'It's fine. I'm over it.'

'Lad, are you getting on the train, or what?' the train man asks.

I look to Felix. 'Well, are you? Or are we going to give this a go?' I ask, my tongue shaking I'm so petrified of his answer.

He puts his hand up for me to help him to standing. Once there, he pulls me to him so our chests are flush, a devilish grin on his face.

'Let the train go,' he says to the man, without losing intense eye contact with me.

I hear the doors close behind us.

'So...' I say, suddenly shy. 'Does this mean we're giving this a go? Like a real go?'

He smiles. 'It means that I'm crazy about the lunatic in the pyjamas, who nearly broke my balls. And if she can forgive me for being a giant dickhead, then I'll gladly spend the rest of my life making it up to her.'

I grin. 'Why are you talking about yourself in the third person?'

'I don't know,' he admits with a grin. 'I started, so I thought I'd roll with it.'

He grabs my face and pulls me slowly into him, our lips meeting in a beautiful union. It contains forgiveness, lust, and love.

'Now we just have to work out where the hell we're going to live.'

He opens his wallet and pulls out a coin. 'Let's flip for it. Heads its Harrow, tails we go wherever you fancy. Either way the other has to be supportive and get a job in McDonalds if they have to. Deal?'

'Are you sure?' I ask.

He smiles fondly down at me. 'As long as we're together, we can tackle anything. I'm happy to start my new life with you, wherever we end up.'

I grin. 'Okay. I'm in.'

He flips the coin in the air and I wait for the fate gods to decide where our next journey takes us. Yet I know that as long as I'm with him we'll be okay.

Even if we drive each other crazy.

## THE END

## ABOUT THE AUTHORS

### Andie M. Long

Andie M. Long tries wherever possible to make people laugh so hard when reading that their families ask them what the hell is going on.

She lives in Sheffield with her long-suffering partner and son.

When not being partner, mother, or writer, she can usually be found on Facebook or walking her whippet, Bella.

---

### Laura Barnard
Laura Barnard writes British quirky laugh out loud romantic comedy.

She lives in Hertfordshire, UK, with her husband and daughter.

In her spare time she enjoys drinking her body weight in tea, cuddling dogs, indulging in cupcakes and chocolate, setting her friends up together (very successfully), indulging in the power nap and reading past her bedtime.

BALLS, TEQUILA AND TEA BAGS

## BALLS – ANDIE M. LONG

Camille Turner has returned to her home town of Rotherham to open her new business, a childrens play centre. She said she left to pursue her education but in reality she was driven away by the antics of fellow pupil Dylan Ball, whose parting shot, a photo of Camille in tight shorts, earned her the nickname Camille Toe.

After swearing revenge as she left the school gates behind her, Camille is reunited with a now older and apologetic Dylan who wants to be friends. She'd tell him to go to Hell but he does genuinely seem sorry. Plus he's also matured into one sexy male.

It's so unfair.

But does Dylan really want to be friends or is it all an act to embarrass her once again?

Includes a Yorkshire/British glossary to teach you some rude slang ;)

GRAB YOUR COPY HERE

## TEQUILA AND TEA BAGS – LAURA BARNARD

Sent to live with her cousin Elsie in the Yorkshire countryside, Rose has only one thing on her mind; joining her friends as a club rep in Mexico. When she hears about a council incentive offering the promise of free flights to the person who clocks the most volunteering hours at the local care home, she's got her plan set. But she doesn't plan on bonding with the old ladies, going after the village bad boy and trying to persuade Elsie not to become a Nun. Soon she's questioning who her real friends are and whether her old life is one she wants to return to. Can the village win her over and will she win the chance to leave it behind? Will she even want to?

GRAB YOUR COPY HERE

ALSO BY ANDIE M. LONG

Andie M. Long

**ANDIE'S BOOKS AVAILABLE HERE**

**www.amazon.com/Andie-M-Long/e/B00HP5D2NK**

**OTHER ROMANTIC COMEDY STORIES FROM ANDIE M. LONG**

Balls Series

Balls

Snow Balls

New Balls Please

Balls Fore

Jingle Balls

Curve Balls

Birthing Balls

Balls up

The Bunk Up - co-written with DH Sidebottom

## **PARANORMAL ROMANTIC COMEDY SERIES**

The Supernatural Dating Agency

Cupid Inc

The Paranormals

ALSO BY LAURA BARNARD

Laura Barnard

Laura's books available here

www.amazon.com/author/laurabarnardbooks

**Other Titles Available**

The Debt & the Doormat Series

The Debt & the Doormat

The Baby & the Bride

Porn Money & Wannabe Mummy

One Month Til I Do Series

Adventurous Proposal

Marrying Mr Valentine

Babes of Brighton Series

Excess Baggage

Love Uncovered

Bagging Alice

## Standalones

Tequila & Tea Bags

Dopey Women

Once Upon a Wish-mas

Cock & Bull

Heath, Cliffs & Wandering Hearts – Young Adult

Sex, Snow & Mistletoe – Short story

Printed in Great Britain
by Amazon